A CHRISTMAS THROUGH TIME

S. A. CARMODY

KMCS PUBLISHING

A Christmas Through Time

© 2025 S. A. Carmody

All rights reserved. No part of this publication may be reproduced, stored in a retrieval system, or transmitted in any form or by any means, electronic, mechanical, photocopying, recording, or otherwise, without the prior written permission of the publisher, except in the case of brief quotations used in reviews or critical articles.

This is a work of fiction. While certain real locations such as Otley, the City of Leeds, and Leeds General Infirmary are referred to, all characters, events, and organisations depicted are entirely fictional. Any resemblance to actual persons, living or dead, or to real events is purely coincidental.

Published by KMCS Publishing

Leeds, United Kingdom

www.kmcspublishing.com

KMCS Publishing is an independent imprint based in Leeds, celebrating original British fiction and cultural heritage.

Print ISBN: 978-1-918259-09-4

eBook ISBN: 978-1-918259-10-0

Printed in the United Kingdom

Cover design by KMCS Publishing

Editing and production by KMCS Publishing

For more titles by S. A. Carmody, visit www.kmcspublishing.com

ARRIVAL

The taxi pulled away, leaving Lucy standing on the pavement with one suitcase and a set of keys that felt too heavy in her hand.

The house loomed above her, three storeys of Victorian stone that had seen better days. Much better days. The window frames needed painting, the guttering sagged on one side, and the front steps were cracked. A bin lay abandoned in the overgrown front garden, half-buried in dead leaves.

Lucy looked up at the grey December sky and then back at the house. Her house now, apparently. A distant relative, someone she'd never even heard of until the solicitor's letter arrived, had died, and the property had gone to her. The solicitor had been perfectly pleasant about it all, handing over the keys in his warm office in Leeds before she'd got a taxi to Otley. He'd explained about probate and utilities and building insurance, and she'd nodded along, understanding perhaps half of it.

'It's a bit run-down, I'm afraid,' he'd said apologetically. 'It's been empty for a long time. But it is structurally sound, the surveyor has assured me, and it's yours now, Ms Patterson. The family connection is rather distant, I'm afraid, several generations removed and through a collateral line. But the genealogists confirmed it, and you're the closest living relative we could trace.'

She picked up her suitcase and climbed the steps. The key stuck in the lock, and she had to jiggle it twice before the door swung open with a protesting creak.

The hallway was dark and smelled of dust and damp. Lucy found a light switch, flipped it. Nothing. Electricity was now at the top of her list of things to sort out. She used her phone torch instead, shining the beam across faded wallpaper and a staircase that rose up into shadows.

Three floors, the solicitor had said. Reception rooms, kitchen, library. Several bedrooms and an attic at the top, that was full of boxes and old furniture that were now all hers.

She closed the door behind her and stood in the silence.

This was it then. Her fresh start, an unexpected inheritance, and an escape from Rachel's sofa, her pitying looks and well-meaning questions about whether she was eating properly, sleeping properly, coping properly.

Lucy set down her suitcase and began to explore.

The front room was shrouded in dust sheets that turned furniture into ghost shapes. She pulled one back and found an ancient sofa, horsehair stuffing leaking from one arm. The windows were tall, reaching nearly to the ceiling, and filthy. Through the grime, she could just make out the street outside and the rooftops of Otley spreading down the hill.

The nursing part of her brain kicked in automatically. Single-glazed windows meant heat loss and the kind of cold that would settle in elderly bones and not let go. She'd seen hypothermia admissions from people living in houses like this. Old people who couldn't afford heating and tried to make do with one bar of an electric fire and layers of cardigans. It never worked, and the cold crept in anyway.

The second reception room held more covered furniture and a piano that was probably hopelessly out of tune. The floor creaked under her feet. Original floorboards, she supposed. Lovely if you liked that sort of thing. Draughty if you had to live here in December.

The kitchen was worse. The units were ancient; there was a cooker that looked like it belonged in a museum, and the wallpaper was peeling in long strips. The floor was lino covered, but it had cracked and yellowed. There was a fridge, but when she opened it, the smell drove her back. She'd need to clean that or throw it out. Either way, it would be added to the list.

The Belfast sink had taps that juddered when she turned them on, and the water ran brown for a full minute before clearing. The back door had a key in the lock, rusted in place. Through the window, she could see a long, narrow garden, completely overgrown, with a shed at the bottom that was listing to one side.

This was a house that needed serious work, along with money she didn't have and skills she definitely didn't possess. Why had the genealogists' search led to her, of all people? Some distant relative had died, leaving no clear heirs, and somehow the trail had ended at her door.

She'd been a name on a family tree, distant and unlikely, plucked from obscurity by researchers tracing collateral lines. The house hadn't been left to her; she'd simply been found.

She found the library at the back of the house, the room that was different from the rest of the place. Wood-panelled walls, floor-to-ceiling bookshelves, a fireplace with an ornate mantelpiece and none of the furniture here was covered. There was a magnificent leather chair, cracked with age, but stunning nonetheless. A desk, solid and imposing, and books, hundreds of them, maybe thousands, packed onto the shelves.

Lucy stepped inside, her footsteps loud on the wooden floor. Her phone torch played across the spines. Medical texts, most of them. Old ones, leather-bound, with titles stamped in faded gold. 'Gray's Anatomy'. 'The Principles and Practice of Medicine'. 'A System of Surgery'. Dates on the spines: 1880, 1882, 1884.

She pulled one out carefully. 'Treatment of Common Fevers' dated 1883. The pages were brittle, spotted with age. The handwriting in the margins, neat and precise, had made notes about symptoms, treatments, dosages. Someone had underlined passages, marked paragraphs with careful asterisks.

There was an urgency in some of the notes. 'Tried this - patient deteriorated'. 'Scarlet fever - three cases this week.' 'Must remember to check pulse more frequently'.

A doctor's library, then. Of her distant relative? She tried to remember what the solicitor had said about the family connection. But he hadn't mentioned medicine, or much of anything really beyond the legal necessities, and these books were far too old to have been used by anyone who had died within under a century, if not longer.

She replaced the book and pulled out another. 'Diseases of Children'. More notes, more underlining. A pressed flower fell out from between the pages, crumbling as it hit the floor. She bent to pick it up, but it disintegrated at her touch.

The desk held more evidence of medical practice. On it stood a brass microscope, tarnished but intact, next to a leather case that opened to reveal surgical instruments, their steel dulled with age. A stack of papers tied with string - patient notes, perhaps? She didn't untie them, not today.

On the mantelpiece sat a clock that had stopped at twenty

past three. A photograph in a silver frame: a stern Victorian couple, the man seated, the woman standing with her hand on his shoulder. Both unsmiling, as was the fashion. The photograph was brown with age; the couple's faces were faded.

Lucy turned, surveying the room. That was when she noticed the bookcase.

It wasn't that it looked different from the others. It had the same dark wood, the same style. But it was slightly off. A fraction of an inch proud of the wall, as if the floor wasn't quite level.

Lucy crossed to it and ran her hand along the edge. There was a gap, barely visible. She pulled at the edge of the bookcase experimentally, but nothing happened.

She tried pushing instead, yet still nothing. There was definitely something odd about it, though. The gap was too regular, too deliberate. A secret compartment? That would be very Victorian. Ridiculous, but very Victorian.

Well, this is a mystery for another day. Right now, she needed to figure out where she was sleeping tonight.

Her phone rang startlingly loud in the quiet house. Rachel's name flashed on the screen.

Lucy answered. 'Hi.'

'Hi yourself. Did you get there okay? How's the house?'

'It's... a house. Victorian and needs a huge amount of work.'

'That's what you said about the last flat you viewed. This one's worse, isn't it?'

'Yes, but it's mine, though so I guess that's something.'

A pause on the other end of the line. Then: 'Luce, are you sure about this? It's Christmas in two weeks. You could come back to ours. Jack won't mind and the kids would love having you here for Christmas Day.'

'I can't keep sleeping on your sofa, Rach. I've been there for two months already.'

'So? You're my best friend. You can stay as long as you need.'

Lucy closed her eyes. Rachel meant well; she always did. But the pity in her voice was hard to bear. Poor Lucy. Divorced at thirty-two, then made redundant and sleeping on her friend's sofa like a teenager who couldn't get her life together.

'I need my own space,' Lucy said, trying to keep her voice light. 'Besides, it'll be good for me. This house is definitely a project that'll keep me busy.'

'You've been busy working yourself into the ground for years. Maybe what you need is to rest and time to process everything that's happened.'

'I'm fine.'

'You're not fine and haven't been fine since Rob left over two years ago, now the divorce is final, and then losing your job on top of everything else…'

'I didn't lose my job. I was made redundant, that's different.'

'Is it?'

Lucy bit down on her irritation. Rachel was her oldest friend. They'd trained together, worked together at Leeds General. Rachel knew her better than almost anyone, which was exactly the problem.

'The ward closed,' Lucy said evenly. 'Because of budget cuts, it wasn't personal.'

'I know, sorry, that came out wrong, but I just worry about you. You've been through so much, and now you're out there in that house, alone, at Christmas…'

'I need to go and call the electricity people to get it connected, and I should find some cleaning supplies, see if I can make the place habitable.'

Another pause. 'Okay. But call me, yeah? If you need anything, or if you just want to talk. Promise?'

'Promise.'

'Love you, Luce.'

'Love you too.'

She ended the call and stood in the library, phone in hand, looking at nothing.

Her divorce was finalised three months ago, and then she was made redundant from Leeds General two months ago. Those were the facts Rachel knew. What she didn't know, what Lucy couldn't quite put into words, was the hollow feeling that had taken up residence in her chest. The sense that she'd somehow failed at every single thing that was supposed to matter.

Thirty-two years old with no job, no husband, and no purpose and now, a half-derelict house in Otley and a suitcase full of clothes that didn't feel like they belonged to her anymore.

She looked around the library. The medical books stared back at her from their shelves. All those careful notes in the margins, some doctor long dead, and yet somehow, his books and notes had remained in the house, in what would have been his library for well over a century. They had never been removed or packed away by her great-uncle or whoever lived in the house before him; they'd just been left as though the doctor might return for them one day like some sort of tribute to a man who was obviously dedicated to his work.

Lucy had been dedicated to her job once, good at assessing and prioritising and staying calm when everything was chaos. Reassuring when holding a frightened patient's hand and explaining things in words they could understand and making sure that she gave the small kindnesses that made hospitals bearable.

When had that stopped being enough?

Lucy turned and left the library, climbing the stairs to the first floor. The bedrooms were in better condition than downstairs, though they still smelled of damp and disuse. She chose the smallest one at the back. It had a double bed with a bare mattress, a wardrobe, and a window overlooking the garden.

She found sheets in the wardrobe, musty but clean enough, and made the bed with practised efficiency. At least nursing had taught her something useful. Hospital corners, tight enough to bounce a coin on.

The bathroom had running water, which was something. Cold water only, but she could boil a kettle if she could find one and make do for tonight.

By the time she'd unpacked her suitcase and arranged her few belongings, it was getting dark outside. The house had no heating controls she could find after a heart-hearted search, so she pulled on an extra jumper, then another, then lay down on the bed fully clothed and stared at the ceiling.

The plaster was cracked in places. There was a light fitting that looked older than she was, and there was water damage in one corner that would need investigating. You couldn't have damp in a bedroom; it caused respiratory problems, especially in the elderly or very young.

She was doing it again, reverting to her familiar habits but assessing the house as if it were a patient. Looking for symptoms, making mental notes about treatment plans.

Outside, she could hear the fresh sounds of her new town, Otley, a place she'd visited but never considered living in, never imagined she had any family connection to at all. Car doors were slamming, a dog was barking, and someone was shouting at their children to go to sleep. Normal family sounds of lives that were full of people who belonged.

Lucy turned on her side and pulled the duvet up to her chin. She got out her phone, keeping one hand under the duvet for warmth, and set up a gas and electricity provider. After Lucy added the tedious details three times and the credit check was successful, the app informed her that her power and heat would be restored shortly, whatever shortly meant and hopefully before Christmas.

She had not properly celebrated Christmas for two years. The first year after Rob left, she'd been too raw. Rachel had invited her over, but she'd claimed a shift at work instead and spent Christmas Day on the ward, grateful for the distraction. Last year, she'd booked a cottage in the Lake District. The photos of an open fire and surrounding space felt so appealing, but the reality had been pure loneliness, cut off from the world and unable to build any sort of fire that didn't extinguish after half an hour.

This year, she'd planned to work again. But then the redundancy notice arrived, and suddenly there was nothing. No job, no plans, no reason to get up in the morning. Other departments in the hospital were desperate for nurses with her experience, but she couldn't bring herself to apply. Eventually, she added her name to the bank rota, only to turn down every shift that came her way. Her confidence had gone, along with what she feared was her ability to do the one thing she'd always done, which was to keep people alive.

Then the solicitor's letter arrived with news that a distant relative, someone she'd never even heard of, had died and left her the property. The letter gave her a house in Otley and the sniff of a chance to start over.

Except she didn't know how to start over. After the separation, she'd gone to see a therapist. The woman had talked about processing the divorce, about being kind to herself, and about the stages of healing. Lucy had nodded along and never gone back. She didn't need therapy; she needed to work harder, be better, prove that she wasn't a failure.

The ward closure had put paid to that plan.

The room was getting colder; she considered going downstairs to have a proper search for a way of heating the place. But moving seemed impossible as the exhaustion that had been building for months pressed down on her, heavy and endless.

Thirty-two years old, her life was in shatters while she lay in a dusty bedroom in a house that was so full of damp and cracks that it looked as if it was about to fall apart too.

Rachel's voice came into her head: 'You're not fine.'

No, she wasn't fine. But she'd say she was and keep saying it until it became true. That's what people did; what nurses did; they kept going, powered through and looked after everyone else while pushing their own needs down deep where nobody could see them.

She'd been good at that. Back on the ward, she'd been the one people came to when they were overwhelmed. The steady one who could handle anything. Code blues, angry relatives, doctors having tantrums, patients dying despite everything she did to save them. She'd handled it all with the same calm competence.

Then one day, she'd woken up and realised she couldn't remember the last time she'd felt anything at all. Not grief, not joy, not even anger. Just a grey flatness that made every moment of her life feel exactly the same.

Rob had noticed eventually. 'You're not here anymore,' he'd said. 'I'm talking to you and you're not even listening. When did you stop caring about us, about our relationship?'

She'd wanted to tell him it wasn't about him. It was about the exhaustion that never lifted, the sense that she was treading water in a sea that kept getting deeper. But she hadn't found the words, and he'd stopped asking, and then he was gone.

The redundancy had almost been a relief. At least it gave her something concrete to grieve. A reason to feel lost that other people could understand, something that she could put into words a lot clearer than the reasons for her and Rob separating.

Lucy closed her eyes. The house felt enormous around her, echoing with all the lives that had been lived here and were gone now. Those medical books in the library, all those careful notes. Someone had sat at that desk and tried to save people with medicine that was hopelessly inadequate. Had they felt this same exhaustion? This sense that no matter how hard you tried, it would never be enough?

Outside, the bells of the nearby parish church rang. An old stone building with graveyards full of people who'd lived and died in houses like this one. Those from days gone by who'd struggled through cold winters and likely died of things that are easily curable now. Pneumonia, infections, or childbirth.

At least modern medicine gave options. Treatments that actually worked. Not like those Victorians, chartered in the books in the library, who had been dosing themselves with mercury and laudanum and hoping for the best. At least they were all now living in a time when a fever or blood poisoning or even a difficult labour wasn't an automatic death sentence.

Tomorrow, she'd start working on her lists with all the practical things that needed doing. She'd keep busy and keep battling the exhaustion that sleep couldn't lift.

But tonight, just for tonight, she let herself feel it. The loneliness, the grief, the fear that she might never find her way back to being whole. The real terror was that this was it now: a cold house, an empty future, and Christmas looming to amplify everything she already felt. Christmas had an infuriating way of making the lonely feel lonelier and the sad feel sadder. It could so easily push the suffering over the edge, into a deeper, darker pit of despair. Christmas was just two weeks away. Most would be with family; with people they loved, and she'd be here in this empty house, trying to convince herself that being alone was the same as being happily independent.

Lucy pulled the duvet tighter and waited for sleep to come.

THE PASSAGE

*L*ucy woke at six, her body clock still stuck on hospital shifts despite two months of unemployment. The bedroom was freezing, her breath visible in the air.

Moving hurt. Every muscle had stiffened overnight on the ancient mattress. I'm getting old, she thought grimly. Thirty-two and already feeling it in her joints like her orthopaedic patients.

Downstairs, the house was no warmer. The cold had settled into the walls, the kind of cold that needed central heating, not just layers of clothing. Hoping desperately that the utilities would be connected today, she searched the unfamiliar cupboards in the hope of finding a jar of abandoned coffee. There was no coffee and no kettle either. Two more things to add to the list.

Instead, she drank water from the tap in the kitchen, metallic tasting but clear enough after she let the water run for a minute. Then she stood in the hallway and looked around, assessing the damage.

Cleaning. That's what she and the house both needed.

Cleaning was practical; it was something to keep her hands busy and her mind occupied. The library seemed the best place to start, as at least that room had potential. Those books might be worth something, and the wood panelling would look stunning after a good dust. Besides, there was that odd bookcase to investigate.

She found cleaning supplies in the cupboard under the stairs. Ancient bottles of furniture polish, a broom with half its bristles missing, cloths so old some disintegrated when she touched them. But it was something to work with, and she wasn't ready to face the shops yet.

The library looked worse in daylight. Cobwebs hung from every corner, and the windows were so filthy she could barely see through them.

Lucy started with the windows, scrubbing at grime that had built up over months, maybe years. Gradually, light began to filter through. Proper light, showing the room as it really was. The wood panelling was darker than she'd thought; the floorboards scarred with age. But there was quality here, proper craftsmanship. Someone had built this room to last.

Next, the desk. Papers tied with string, all of them brittle with age. Medical notes with names, dates, symptoms. 'Mrs Fletcher, age 42, presented with fever and confusion.' 'Young Timothy Dawson, age 7, severe croup.' Brief, factual descriptions. No outcomes were recorded, suggesting they hadn't been good.

Victorian medicine seemed to rely on bloodletting, leeches, and hoping for the best. During her training, she'd done a history module, learning about the development of nursing from Victorian times onwards. Florence Nightingale and hygiene. Lister and antisepsis. The gradual understanding that cleanliness mattered, that infections weren't caused by 'bad air' but by actual physical organisms you could prevent with soap and water.

But knowing the theory and seeing these notes, about real patients who'd suffered using treatments that ranged from useless to actively harmful, that was different. A seven-year-old with what was almost certainly diphtheria, who had most likely died choking, unable to breathe. There was nothing anyone could have done in 1880-whatever. But now? A simple vaccination would have saved him.

Lucy set the papers aside carefully and moved to the bookshelves.

Books came off in stacks. Medical texts, most of them, but also novels. Dickens, Trollope, George Eliot. A complete set of Shakespeare. Poetry by Tennyson and Browning. Someone had been well-read, educated and interested in more than just medicine.

Working her way along the third shelf, she noticed the bookcase again. The one that sat slightly proud of the wall.

Curious now, she pulled all the books off it. Leather-bound volumes, heavy and musty. 'A Practical Treatise on Surgical Operations' from 1882. 'The Diagnosis of Nervous Diseases' from 1883. 'Common Ailments and Their Treatment' from 1884.

Behind the books, the wooden backing looked normal. The solid panels had been professionally fitted. But there had to be something because of the gap at the edge, the way it stood away from the wall; it all pointed to something deliberate.

Lucy ran her hands over the wood, feeling for catches, hidden mechanisms. There was nothing obvious. Perhaps she was imagining things; she was just about to give up when her fingers found it. A small lever tucked behind where the 1884 textbook had stood. Recessed in the wood, almost invisible unless you knew to look for it.

With her heart suddenly thumping, Lucy gripped the lever and pulled.

Something clicked deep in the mechanism. The bookcase shuddered, then swung smoothly outward on hidden hinges, revealing a narrow opening in the wall behind.

'Oh my God,' Lucy said aloud.

A passage. An actual secret passage with stone-lined walls, so narrow in parts that she'd have to turn sideways if she walked through it. There was darkness beyond, though she could see the faint outline of what seemed to be a door at the far end.

This was absurd. Secret passages didn't exist in real life. They existed in Enid Blyton novels and Scooby-Doo cartoons. Not in actual Victorian houses in Otley.

Lucy stood in front of the opening, her mind racing. Priest hole, surely. Catholics hiding during persecution. But wasn't that in the sixteenth century, not the Victorian era? Why would someone build a secret passage?

There was only one way to find out.

Getting her phone from her pocket, she turned on the torch and stepped into the passage.

The air inside was different. Not stale, as she'd expected, but fresh. Almost moving, like there was ventilation somewhere. The floor was stone, worn smooth in the centre where possibly countless feet had walked. The walls were close on either side, the ceiling low enough that she had to duck slightly.

Ten feet in length, perhaps. That's all it was, a very short passage connecting... what? Two rooms? Two houses?

At the end, was another door. A wooden one, old but well-maintained, with a polished brass handle, and no lock that she could see.

Lucy hesitated, her hand on the handle. Was she entering someone's house and trespassing? But then again, the passage had opened from her library, so surely it was still her property? Surely, she had a right to see where it led.

Before she could talk herself out of it, she pushed the handle down and opened the door.

Light flooded in. Bright morning light, much brighter than the room she had left had been. Blinking, Lucy stepped through and then stopped dead.

It was exactly the same library as the one she'd left. It had the same dimensions, the same layout, the same wood panelling, and yet, everything was different.

The furniture was gleaming, polished and cared for. Pristine books were on the shelves, with their leather bindings rich and colourful. A fire burned in the grate, warming the room. The desk was tidy, with papers stacked neatly, an inkwell and pen laid out ready for use. Gaslight fixtures jutted from the walls, brass and ornate, though unlit in the morning brightness.

No dust, neglect, or decay. It was as if she'd stepped into the same room, but fifty years earlier.

It was impossible, obviously impossible. Definitely an hallucination, a stress-induced psychotic break. Extreme stress could cause visual hallucinations and make people see things that weren't there. Divorce, redundancy, isolation, they could all trigger it. Her mental health placement had covered this.

Except it felt real. The warmth from the fire, the smell of burning wood and furniture polish, the textures under her feet, they all felt real.

Lucy took another step into the room, looking around wildly. The curtains were different, dark green velvet instead of faded cotton. The rug under her feet was thick wool, intricately patterned. Some of the books were the same as in her library; others were different titles, or the same titles but older editions.

Voices drifted from somewhere in the house. A woman was speaking, though her words were indistinct. Then, the sound of footsteps on stairs.

Panic hit her suddenly. Someone was here, in this house, wherever this house was, and she was trespassing, standing in someone else's library, one that felt very out of place.

Before she could move or retreat through the passage, a man appeared in the doorway.

He stopped dead, staring at her.

He was in his mid-thirties, with dark hair that was neatly combed, dark eyes that were wide with shock. He wore a waistcoat over a white shirt, his sleeves rolled to the elbows, with a stethoscope that hung around his neck, the earpieces resting against his chest. His hands were clean, his nails trimmed short.

A doctor, Lucy's brain supplied automatically or, at the very least, a medical professional.

'Who are you?' he demanded. His voice was educated, precise. Angry but controlled. 'How did you get into my house?'

Lucy gaped at him. At his clothes, which looked like a costume but weren't. Then, at the room behind him, which was her library but wasn't. The stethoscope was made of wood and rubber, not plastic.

'Your house?' The words came out strangled. 'This is my house. I inherited it from…'

'This house has been in my family for three generations.' His voice was flat, brooking no argument. 'I don't know what game you're playing, madam, but you're trespassing.' His eyes travelled down to her jeans, her trainers, her fleece jumper. 'And your attire is… what on earth are you wearing?'

Another figure appeared behind him before Lucy could answer. A woman, older, perhaps sixty. Her grey hair pulled back in a tight bun, and wearing a long black dress with a white apron. Her face was lined, stern.

'Dr Ashworth,' the woman said, her voice sharp with alarm. 'Shall I fetch the constable?'

'I think that might be...'

'No!' Lucy backed toward the passage. 'I'm sorry, I didn't mean to... I'll just go.'

'How did you get in?' The doctor, Dr Ashworth, moved forward. 'The doors are all locked. The windows are secure. Did you break in? Are you here to steal?'

'No! I came through the...' Lucy gestured behind her at the passage. 'Through there. From my house, my library. I just opened the door and...'

Both of them stared at her as if she'd lost her mind. Perhaps she had and was still upstairs in bed, having a very vivid nightmare brought on by stress and cold and sleeping in a strange house.

'Through the wall,' Dr Ashworth said slowly. 'You came through the wall.'

'Through the passage! There's a passage behind the bookcase, it opened when I pulled the lever, and I just walked through, and now I'm here, and I don't know how, but this is my house, or it was my house, and...'

'Mrs Barker,' the doctor said, not taking his eyes off Lucy. 'Perhaps fetch the smelling salts instead of the constable. This woman appears to be suffering from some form of mania.'

'I'm not mad!' Lucy's voice rose, panic making it sharp. 'I'm a nurse, I work at Leeds General Infirmary, or I did until two months ago, and I inherited this house from a great-uncle, and there's a passage behind the bookcase, and I don't know what's happening, but I'm not crazy!'

The doctor's expression changed slightly. Less anger,

more concern. A medical professional assessing a patient. 'You're a nurse.'

'Yes, with twelve years' experience on medical and surgical wards. I know how this sounds, but I promise you, I'm not hallucinating. Or I don't think I am. Though I suppose if I were, I wouldn't know, would I?' Babbling now, words tumbling over each other. 'Look, I'll just go. Back through the passage to where I came from. I'm sorry for disturbing you.'

'Wait,' the doctor said, but Lucy was already turning.

She just had to go back through the passage, and this would stop, this madness would end, and she could call Rachel and admit that yes, actually, she wasn't coping, and yes, she probably needed help.

Lucy plunged into the passage, pulling the door shut behind her, allowing the darkness to swallow her. Her hands found the stone walls, cold and solid, and she stumbled forward, desperate to get out, to get back to reality.

The bookcase stood open where she'd left it. Daylight beyond, grey and familiar. Bursting through into her dusty, cold, neglected library, Lucy stood there breathing hard, her heart hammering against her ribs.

What just happened?

The passage was still there and the bookcase still open; she could see the darkness beyond it, unchanged.

Lucy stared at it, at the impossible thing that couldn't exist but did.

A secret passage. Leading to... what? Another version of the house? A different time? An elaborate hallucination?

Her hands were shaking. Clasping them together, she tried to steady herself.

She searched for a medical explanation. There had to be a medical explanation. Stress could cause hallucinations, as could sleep deprivation, hypothermia, or even low blood sugar. When had she last eaten? Yesterday lunchtime? That was nearly twenty-four hours ago. No wonder her brain was malfunctioning.

But it had felt real. The warmth of the fire, the smell of wood smoke, the texture of the rug under her feet. The doctor's voice, angry and then concerned. The woman's gasp of shock.

Lucy walked slowly to the desk and sat down in the leather chair. Creaking under her weight. Patient notes lay where she'd left them on the desk. 'Mrs Fletcher, age 42.' 'Young Timothy Dawson, age 7.'

The name, Dr Ashworth. That was the name on one of the books; she was sure of it. Standing, Lucy went to the pile of medical texts she'd removed from the bookcase. There. 'Common Ailments and Their Treatment'. No author listed on the spine, but she opened it anyway. Inside the cover, written in careful script: 'Property of Dr James Ashworth, MRCS'.

The same name the woman had used. Dr Ashworth.

Maybe she'd seen the name subconsciously, and her stressed brain had incorporated it into the hallucination.

Except the man had been wearing Victorian clothes and had a Victorian stethoscope. He had spoken like someone from another era, his words formal and precise, and the room had been full of light because the windows were clean, because someone was maintaining the house, because it wasn't abandoned and neglected.

Standing up abruptly, Lucy shook her head. This was all ridiculous. Secret passages didn't lead to other times. That was fantasy, science fiction, impossible.

But the passage was there. Solid and real and there was only one way to find out if the rest was real too.

Before she could lose her nerve, Lucy walked back to the

opening. The passage stretched away into shadow. At the far end, just visible, stood the wooden door.

Terrified, Lucy stepped into the passage again. The walk seemed longer this time. Each step deliberate and each breath loud in the confined space. At the door, she paused. What would she find? The same library? A different one? Nothing at all?

There was only one way to find out. Taking a breath, Lucy opened the door.

The same bright library greeted her. The fire was still burning, and the books still gleaming. But this time, the room was empty. There was no doctor or woman in there. Just the space itself, warm and maintained and utterly impossible.

Very still, Lucy listened. Voices somewhere above, muffled by distance. Then footsteps. Someone was definitely here, living here, going about their day.

Moving quietly, she crossed to the desk. There were papers, letters and also medical notes written in that same precise hand she'd seen in the medical texts in her own library.

'Dear Dr Henderson,' one began. 'I write to consult you regarding a patient of mine, a girl of fourteen years who presents with symptoms that perplex me...'

The date at the top of the letter: 11th December 1885. Lucy sat down hard in the nearest chair.

One hundred and forty years ago. The passage had taken her back one hundred and forty years.

Except that was impossible. Time travel didn't exist; it simply couldn't exist because it violated every law of physics she'd ever heard of.

But here she was. In a library that was hers but wasn't, in a house that existed in two times at once, reading letters written before her great-grandparents were born.

'This isn't happening,' Lucy said aloud. Her voice sounded strange in the quiet room. 'I'm having a breakdown, a stress-induced psychotic break. I need to go home and call someone. Rachel. I need to call Rachel.'

But she didn't move. Instead, she looked around the library, taking in every detail. Medical books on the shelves, titles she recognised. 'Gray's Anatomy', though an earlier edition than the one she'd studied from. 'Diseases of the Heart and Blood Vessels'. 'The Principles of Surgery'.

On the mantelpiece, that same photograph she'd seen in her own library. The stern Victorian couple. But here, the silver frame was polished and the photograph clear and sharp.

A clock ticked quietly on the wall. It was twenty past nine. The fire crackled, and from outside, she could hear horses and their clip-clop of hooves on cobblestones.

Real. It was all real; it had to be. Standing, Lucy walked to the window, drew back the curtain slightly and looked out.

She saw the same street as hers with the same houses opposite, the same layout. But it was all different. A horse and cart stood outside one house where a man was loading boxes. A woman in a long dress and bonnet walked past, carrying a basket. There were no cars or telephone wires, no satellite dishes or double glazing, none of the things that marked a modern street.

It was Victorian Otley. She was actually looking at Victorian Otley.

The sound of footsteps on the stairs was getting closer. Dropping the curtain, Lucy looked around wildly for somewhere to hide. She was in someone else's house, intruding on their life, and wearing impossible clothes from an impossible future.

The curtains, she thought, jumping behind them. The

thought was absurd and childish, but there was no time for anything else.

Lucy ducked behind the heavy velvet drapes just as the door opened.

'...not sleeping properly,' a woman's voice said. It sounded like the voice of Mrs Barker, the woman from earlier. 'Not eating properly. It's been a year since Mrs Ashworth passed, God rest her, and you've not taken a day's rest.'

'I can't.' The doctor's voice. Dr Ashworth. He sounded weary, Lucy noticed. So tired, it roughened his words. 'The fever cases are increasing. The Dawson child is critical. If I rest, then more people will die.'

'And if you don't rest, you'll die. Begging your pardon, sir, but you look dreadful.'

A pause. Then: 'I know. But what else can I do, Mrs Barker? I'm the only doctor for two miles. If I don't see them, who will?'

'Dr Henderson...'

'Is seventy years old and half-blind. I'll manage as I always have.'

'That woman,' Mrs Barker said abruptly. 'The strange one. Do you think I imagined her too?'

'I don't know, perhaps we both did. The mind plays tricks when you're exhausted.'

Pressed against the wall behind the curtain, Lucy barely breathed. Through the gap in the fabric, she could just see them. The doctor stood by the desk and picked up his medical bag. His hands shook slightly. Mrs Barker was right; he looked dreadful. Incredibly thin, with dark shadows under his eyes, his skin pale.

A man working himself to death, Lucy thought. Just like half the doctors she'd worked with and much like herself, if she was honest, before the redundancy had forced her to stop.

'You should eat something before you go,' Mrs Barker said. 'I've made porridge.'

'No time. I need to check on the Dawson boy. His fever was 104 last night.'

'Dr Ashworth…'

But he was already gone, striding out of the room with his bag in hand. A moment later, Lucy heard the front door close.

Mrs Barker stood alone in the library, shaking her head. 'Work yourself into an early grave, you will,' she muttered. Then she too left, her footsteps fading toward the back of the house.

Emerging from behind the curtain, Lucy's legs shook. She needed to go back through the passage, back to 2025, back to where things made sense. Except nothing made sense to her anymore.

Crossing to the passage quickly, before anyone could return, Lucy stepped into the darkness and pulled the door shut behind her.

Back in her dusty library, the modern world felt both alien and comforting. Cold, neglected, falling apart, but real. Understandable and normal.

Closing the bookcase carefully, Lucy stood staring at it.

In Victorian Otley, there was a doctor named James Ashworth who was working himself to death, and there was a passage that connected them across one hundred and forty years.

'Right,' Lucy said to the empty room. 'Right. Okay. What the hell do I do now?'

INVESTIGATION

For an hour, Lucy paced the library. Back and forth, back and forth, wearing a track in the dust on the floorboards. Her mind raced through possibilities, each more absurd than the last.

Hallucination seemed most likely. Except hallucinations didn't persist when you left and came back. They didn't maintain consistent details, and as far as she was aware, they didn't smell of wood smoke and furniture polish.

Carbon monoxide poisoning, perhaps? The house was old; the heating system was ancient. Maybe there was a leak somewhere, causing her to see things that weren't there. But no, carbon monoxide made you sleepy and confused, not able to hold coherent conversations with Victorian doctors.

Brain tumour? God, that was a cheerful thought. Except brain tumours caused gradual changes, not sudden transportations to other time periods.

Nervous breakdown, then. Complete psychotic break with reality. Except she felt fine. Tired, stressed, and she'd definitely felt down. But not hearing voices or seeing things that vanished when she looked away.

The bookcase stood closed, innocent-looking. Just a bookcase with nothing special about it at all. Except for the passage behind it, which enabled time travel!

Lucy stopped pacing and stared at it. There was only one way to prove this one way or another, and that was to do a proper investigation, thoroughly and meticulously. Gather evidence, test the hypothesis, draw conclusions, do a real scientific investigation, somehow. Because that was a perfectly normal thing to do on a Tuesday morning.

She crossed to the bookcase and pulled the lever. The mechanism clicked; the bookcase swung open. The passage waited, dark and uninviting. Taking a deep breath, Lucy stepped inside once again.

The walk to the far door felt longer this time. Perhaps because she knew what waited on the other side and because part of her hoped it would be different this time, normal, just another room in her own house in her own time.

At the door, she paused with her hand on the handle, took a deep breath and then opened it.

Again, there was the bright Victorian library with the crackling fire and books gleaming. Everything exactly as it had been before.

Lucy stepped through and closed the door carefully behind her. The room was empty, silent except for the clock ticking on the mantelpiece and the fire in the grate. Somewhere in the house, she could hear movement. Footsteps on the floor above, the distant clatter of pots from what must be the kitchen.

Right, investigation time. Gather evidence and find proof that this was real or proof that she'd completely lost her mind. Either way, she needed to know.

Moving quietly, Lucy began a systematic examination of the room. The books were first, and she pulled volumes from the shelves, checking publication dates, publishers, edition numbers. All printed during Victorian times but felt new.

Next, the desk. Letters, bills, medical notes. Everything dated December 1885. Handwriting consistent across all documents. Detail that would be impossible to fake in a hallucination. An invoice from a medical supply company in Leeds. Then a letter from another doctor asking for a consultation. Patient notes recording symptoms, treatments, outcomes.

Lucy picked up one of the patient files. 'Sarah Mitchell, age 19, presented with fever and rash. Probable scarlet fever. Prescribed bed rest, cool compresses, liquids. Temperature 103 degrees.' Notes in the margin: 'Husband states three neighbours ill with similar symptoms. Possible outbreak?'

Real patients with severe illnesses and terror in those brief, clinical sentences.

On the mantelpiece, Lucy examined the photograph more closely. The stern Victorian couple stared out at her. The man seated, perhaps sixty, with impressive side-whiskers and a dark suit. The woman stood, her hand on his shoulder, her dress high-necked and severe. Neither smiled. Behind them, Lucy could just make out wallpaper with a floral pattern.

A small brass nameplate sat beside the photograph. She picked it up, angling it to catch the light. 'Dr James Ashworth, MRCS, LSA. General Practitioner. Consultations by appointment.'

James Ashworth. The man who'd confronted her earlier, the same doctor with the exhausted eyes and shaking hands.

Again, footsteps on the stairs. Getting closer.

Lucy looked around frantically. The curtains again? No, too obvious. Mrs Barker would notice if they were disturbed again. Behind the door? Too risky. Under the desk?

She dropped to her knees and crawled into the desk's footwell, pulling the chair in after her. Not ideal, but it would have to do. At least from here she could see into the room through the gap between the chair legs.

The door opened. Two people entered. James Ashworth and an older man, white-haired and stooped, carrying a black medical bag similar to James's.

'I'm telling you, Henderson, I'm fine,' James was saying. 'Mrs Barker is overreacting. She always does, she is my housekeeper, not my mother.'

'Mrs Barker is worried about you. As am I.' The older man's voice was gruff, authoritative. 'Sit down. Let me examine you.'

'I don't have time for this. The Dawson boy is still critical, and I have three more house calls to.'

'Sit down!'

With obvious reluctance, James sat in the leather armchair by the fire. Henderson set down his bag and pulled out a stethoscope, pressing it to James's chest.

'Breathe in. Hold it. Out. Again.'

Silence while Henderson listened. From her hiding place, Lucy watched James's face. He looked annoyed, impatient, but underneath that was something else. Fear, perhaps. The fear of someone who knows something is wrong but doesn't want it confirmed.

'Your heart rate is elevated,' Henderson said finally. 'When did you last sleep properly?'

'I sleep.'

'When did you last sleep through the night without being called out?'

James didn't answer.

'When did you last eat a full meal? And I don't mean a piece of toast grabbed between patients. I mean an actual meal with three courses with you sitting down throughout.'

'I eat enough.'

'You're thin as a rail. Your hands are shaking, and your

eyes are sunken. James, you're killing yourself. You do understand that don't you?'

'What I understand,' James said tightly, 'is that I have patients who need me. The fever outbreak is getting worse. If I don't treat them, who will? You? You can barely see well enough to read prescriptions anymore.'

'That's unkind.'

'But true and I'm not trying to be cruel, Henderson. I'm being realistic. There are two doctors in this part of Otley. You and me. You're seventy-three and half-blind so that leaves me. So yes, I'm tired because I'm working too hard. But what choice do I have?'

Henderson was quiet for a moment. Then he said, more gently: 'The choice to take care of yourself. Eat, sleep and accept that you cannot save everyone, and killing yourself in the attempt won't bring Eleanor back.'

James flinched as if he'd been struck. 'Don't.'

'Someone needs to say it. You've been punishing yourself since she died. Working yourself into the ground as if exhaustion is penance. But Eleanor wouldn't have wanted this, you know she wouldn't.'

'Eleanor is dead.' The words were flat, lifeless. 'What she wanted is irrelevant.'

'Is it? Because I think if she could see you now, she'd be furious. She'd tell you to stop being a muttonhead and take care of yourself. She'd probably throw something at you to shock you into rest.'

Despite everything, James almost smiled. 'She did have excellent aim.'

'She did. Remember when she threw that book at you for missing her birthday dinner?'

'Yes, it caught me right on the temple and raised a bruise the size of a sovereign.' The smile faded. 'I was in surgery with a man who had a strangulated hernia. I couldn't leave him.'

'And she understood. She always understood. But she also made you promise to come home and eat something, and you did. You took care of yourself because she insisted on it. Now she's gone and you've decided caring for yourself doesn't matter anymore.'

'It doesn't. Not compared to my patients.'

'Your patients will get a new doctor if you die. You, however, will be permanently dead. Which outcome seems preferable?'

Lucy, cramped under the desk, watched James's face. She saw the stubbornness there, the refusal to accept what he clearly knew was true, and also saw the grief underlying everything, the way his jaw tightened when Henderson mentioned Eleanor.

'I'll be more careful,' James said finally. 'I'll try to eat better and sleep more. Satisfied?'

'No. But it's a start.' Henderson stood, picking up his bag. 'I'm serious, James. If you don't slow down, your heart will give out. You're heading for collapse and quite possibly before the end of the year.'

'Cheerful diagnosis. Thank you so much.'

'I'm not joking. Heart failure because of exhaustion is real. I've seen it happen to men your age who are working too hard, ignoring the warning signs. One day they simply drop dead. I don't want that to be you.'

'Then let's hope the fever outbreak ends soon. Once that's managed, I'll rest. I promise.'

Henderson didn't look convinced, but he nodded. 'I'm holding you to that and I'll be checking on you. If Mrs Barker tells me you're still skipping meals and working through the night, I'll tell the Medical Society you're unfit to practice.'

'You wouldn't dare.'

'Try me.' Henderson moved toward the door, then paused. 'James, I say this because I care about you. Because I have worked with you since you qualified, and I'm proud of the doctor you've become. Don't throw that away and don't throw your life away. There's more to living than medicine.'

'Is there? Because from where I'm standing, medicine is all I have left.'

Henderson sighed. 'That's what worries me.' He left, closing the door behind him.

James sat alone by the fire, staring into the flames. After a moment, he leaned forward, head in his hands. His shoulders shook once, twice. Then he straightened, took a deep breath, and stood.

'Right,' he said to the empty room. 'The Dawson boy, then Mrs Smith and onto the Miller family. Then perhaps, if there's time, I'll eat something to keep Henderson happy.'

He picked up his medical bag and walked out.

Lucy waited until his footsteps faded. Then she crawled out from under the desk, her legs cramping. She stood slowly, looking around the library.

Before the end of the year, Henderson had said. Heart failure because a young man was working himself to death.

Moving quickly now, Lucy searched for more information. The desk drawers held bills, correspondence, and medical journals. One drawer held personal items. A woman's handkerchief, embroidered with flowers, along with a lock of dark hair tied with a ribbon. Next to it was a wedding photograph, much smaller than the one on the mantelpiece. James Ashworth and a woman, both younger, both smiling. The woman was pretty, with kind eyes and a gentle smile.

Eleanor. It had to be.

The photograph was dated on the back: 'James and Eleanor Ashworth, 14th June 1883. Our wedding day.'

Two and a half years ago. Henderson had said it had been a year since she had died. So, she'd died in 1884, age... Lucy did the maths. If they were married in 1883 and she was, what, mid-twenties in the photograph? Then she'd died at maybe twenty-seven, twenty-eight. Young. Far too young.

Lucy replaced the photograph carefully and closed the drawer. Then she left, back through the passage, back to her cold, dusty library in 2025.

The moment she emerged; she grabbed her laptop from her suitcase and connected to the internet using her phone as a hotspot. She sighed with relief as three signal bars appeared. Good enough. Sitting at the dusty desk, Lucy searched: 'Dr James Ashworth Otley 1885'.

The first result was a local history website. She clicked through.

'Dr James Ashworth (1850-1885) was a general practitioner in Otley, Yorkshire. He studied medicine at Edinburgh University, qualifying in 1873, and took over his father's practice in Otley in 1875. He married Eleanor Grace Henderson in 1883. Mrs Ashworth died of pneumonia in November 1884, aged 28.'

Lucy scrolled down.

'Dr Ashworth died on 25th December 1885, aged 35. The cause of death was recorded as heart failure, likely due to exhaustion and malnutrition. Contemporary accounts describe him as having worked himself to the point of collapse following his wife's death. He was found dead in his surgery on Christmas morning. He left no children.'

Lucy read the paragraph again, and then again. Heart failure, exhaustion, and malnutrition. Found dead on Christmas morning. It was everything Henderson had warned him about and everything Mrs Barker had worried about. It was all going to happen.

In two weeks, James Ashworth would collapse in his surgery and die. Alone. On Christmas Day.

Unless.

Lucy stared at the screen. Unless what? Unless she could change it? How? She was a nurse from 2025 with no credentials in 1885, no standing, no authority. What could she possibly do?

But she couldn't just let him die. Could she? Knowing what was going to happen, seeing him work himself toward collapse, watching him refuse to take care of himself. How could she just walk away?

'This is insane,' Lucy said aloud. 'Time travel, Victorian doctors and changing history. This is completely insane.'

But she was already pulling up more search results, looking for more information. What happened after James died? Who took over his practice? Were his patients cared for?

Another local history site had the answer: 'Following Dr Ashworth's untimely death, the practice was taken over by Dr William Fletcher, who arrived in Otley in January 1886. Dr Fletcher served the community for the next forty years, retiring in 1926.'

So, the patients were fine; someone else simply took over. The world continued without James Ashworth, who had died on Christmas Day, alone at the age of thirty-five.

Lucy closed the laptop and sat back in the chair. Outside, Otley went about its business. Cars passing, people living their normal lives in the present day. While ten feet away, through a passage in the wall, a man in 1885 was slowly killing himself and didn't know he had two weeks left.

She should leave it alone. History had happened, and James Ashworth died on Christmas Day 1885. That was a fact, recorded and documented. You couldn't change history. Could you?

But if the passage existed, if time travel was real, then maybe history wasn't as fixed as everyone thought. Maybe it could be changed, and she could possibly save him. Or maybe she'd make things worse. Paradoxes, butterfly effects, all those things from science fiction. Change one thing, and the whole timeline collapses.

Except she was a nurse, and saving people was what she did; it was what she'd been trained for. And James Ashworth was a patient, whether he knew it or not. A patient heading for cardiac arrest due to malnutrition and exhaustion. The treatment was obvious: proper nutrition, rest, stress reduction.

Lucy stood and walked back to the bookcase. The passage was still open, still waiting. She had two weeks to decide what to do.

But first, she needed to know more. About James, about 1885, about what she was dealing with. Research first. Then decisions.

Closing the bookcase, Lucy returned to her laptop and started searching properly. Dr James Ashworth. Eleanor Ashworth. Otley 1885. Medical practices. Victorian medicine. She kept everything she could find just in case she decided to do something about it.

THE SECOND MEETING

*L*ucy spent the rest of the day in a haze of research. Victorian medicine, medical ethics, the complications of malnutrition and exhaustion. Heart failure in young men. Along with the historical records of Otley. She searched for every detail about James Ashworth and the world he lived in.

By evening, she'd made a decision. She had to go back and talk to him properly, to explain what was happening. Maybe he'd listen, or maybe he wouldn't, or maybe he'd see her again and drop dead of a heart attack there and then out of fright.

The sun had set by the time she stepped through the passage again. On the other side, the library glowed with gaslight. Two wall sconces cast a warm, flickering light across the room. A single lamp burned on the desk, where James Ashworth sat writing, his dark head bent over papers.

Lucy stepped through and closed the door quietly behind her. For a moment, she just watched him as hand moved across the page in quick, precise strokes. Patient notes, possibly. Recording symptoms, treatments, outcomes. The work never stopped.

He must have heard her, though, because he looked up suddenly. His eyes widened. The pen fell from his hand, spattering ink across the paper.

'You,' he said. Stood abruptly, nearly knocking over his chair. 'You're real, then. I thought I'd imagined you this morning. The exhaustion, the stress. Henderson said I was hallucinating.'

'I'm real.' Lucy stayed where she was, hands visible, non-threatening. 'And I need to explain something that's going to sound completely mad.'

'Madder than a woman appearing in my library wearing trousers and claiming to have walked through a wall?' His voice was dry, but his hands gripped the edge of the desk. 'I'm not sure that's possible.'

'Trust me, it gets madder.'

'Wonderful. Just what I needed today. On top of three pneumonia cases and the Dawson boy taking a turn for the worse.' He sat down again slowly, never taking his eyes off her. 'Very well. Explain. What are you? Some kind of advanced burglar? An actress playing an elaborate prank? A patient escaped from an asylum?'

'None of those. I'm exactly what I told you. A nurse. My name is Lucy Patterson, and I inherited this house from a distant relative. When I moved in yesterday, I found a passage behind the bookcase. When I walked through it, I ended up here. In your time.'

'My time.' He said it flatly. 'As opposed to your time, which is...?'

'2025. One hundred and forty years in the future.'

Silence. James stared at her. Then he laughed, short and humourless. 'You're quite unwell, aren't you? This is some kind of elaborate delusion. Folie à deux, perhaps, given that

Mrs Barker also saw you. Or possibly I'm the one hallucinating and you're a symptom of complete mental collapse.' He rubbed his eyes tiredly. 'Either way, you need medical care. Or I do. Possibly we both do.'

'I can prove it.'

'Prove that you're from the future? How exactly do you propose to do that?'

Lucy pulled her phone from her pocket. 'With this.'

James looked at the small rectangle of glass and metal in her hand. 'With that. Which is...?'

'A telephone. Well, a mobile telephone. A portable communication device. But it does much more than that.' She tapped the screen, bringing it to life. The sudden glow made James jerk backward onto his chair. 'It's also a camera, a computer, a library, a map, and about a thousand other things.'

'It's glowing,' James said faintly. 'You're holding a glowing rectangle.'

'It's a screen. Light-emitting diodes. LED technology.' She crossed to the desk and set the phone down in front of him. 'Look. Don't touch it yet just look.'

Cautiously, James leaned forward. Her home screen showed a photograph she'd taken last month of Rachel's garden. He stared at it for a long moment.

'That's a photograph,' he said slowly. 'In colour. Moving slightly as you shift the rectangle.'

'It's called a smartphone. This particular one is an iPhone, but there are other brands. Nearly everyone in my time has one.' Lucy swiped through to her photos. 'Look. These are all photographs I've taken.'

James bent closer, peering at the images. Rachel's children playing in the garden. The view from Lucy's old flat in Leeds. A sunset over the Pennines. His breathing had quickened.

'The quality,' he whispered. 'It's extraordinary. Better than any photograph I've ever seen and the colours. How is this possible?'

'Digital photography. The camera captures light using electronic sensors rather than chemical processes. These photos aren't physical objects, they're data. Information stored electronically.' She swiped to a video she'd taken of Rachel's cat. 'Watch this.'

She pressed play. The cat moved on the screen, batting at a toy mouse. After a few seconds, you could hear Rachel laughing in the background.

James pushed his chair back so fast it nearly toppled. 'That's impossible. Photographs don't move and they certainly don't produce sound.'

'In 2025, they do. This is called video. Moving images with sound. Everyone can record them on these phones.' Lucy picked up the device and turned on the torch function. Bright white light flooded across the desk. 'This is just one of its features. Electric light, powered by a battery inside the phone. No wires, no gas, no flames.'

'Electric light that fits in your hand.' James was standing now, backing away slowly. 'This is a trick. Some kind of stage magic. Mirrors and wires and...'

'No tricks, just technology. One hundred and forty years of technological development.' She turned off the torch and opened her word app, quickly searching for documents she'd sent to her phone earlier. 'Otley Yorkshire'. She handed him the phone. 'Here, read this. It's about Otley. Your town, but from my time.'

James took the phone gingerly, holding it as if it might explode. His eyes scanned the screen, widening as he read. 'This is about Otley. But it mentions things that don't exist. A bypass. Industrial estates. A railway station that closed in 1965.' He looked up at her. 'How is this possible?'

'Because it's from the future. My time. It can show you

anything you want to know, but here, in this time, I can only show you what I've saved to the device, no 5g you see.'

'Five what?'

'Long story but the entire collected knowledge of humanity is accessible through this device.' Lucy took the phone back and searched through her Word docs and brought up her section on Victorian medicine and showed him the results. 'Look. Articles about medical practices in your time. Written by historians in mine.'

James read silently. His face had gone very pale. After a moment, he sat down heavily in his chair.

'This describes my work,' he said quietly. 'The tools I use as well as the treatments I prescribe. Written as if they're historical curiosities. Primitive attempts at healing.' He looked up at her. 'If this is a delusion, it's remarkably detailed.'

'It's not a delusion. I'm really from 2025. The passage really connects our times, and I really am standing in your library, showing you a smartphone, having a conversation that should be impossible.'

'Why?' The question came out rough. 'Why is this happening? What's the purpose of this passage? Why you? Why me? Why now?'

'I don't know. I've been asking myself the same questions all day.' Lucy pulled out the desk chair and sat down facing him. 'But there's something else I need to tell you. Something I found when I researched you in my time.'

His jaw tightened. 'Go on.'

'I found historical records about you. About Dr James Ashworth of Otley.' She paused, searching for the right words. 'I found out when you died.'

The colour drained from his face. 'When I died.'

'Yes.'

'Not if. When.'

'Well, we all die eventually, but yes.'

A long silence. Outside, Lucy could hear horses passing on the street. The clock on the mantelpiece ticked steadily. The gaslight flickered.

'When?' James asked finally. His voice was perfectly controlled, but his hands shook slightly as he set the phone down on the desk.

'Christmas Day. This year, just two weeks from now. The historical record says you died of heart failure because you worked yourself to death after your wife passed. They found you in your surgery on Christmas morning.'

James closed his eyes. Drew in a breath and let it out slowly. When he opened his eyes again, they were very dark in the lamplight.

'Well,' he said. 'That's remarkably specific and unfortunately, believable.'

'I'm sorry. I didn't know if I should tell you, but I couldn't not tell you. Not when I know what's going to happen.'

'Why did you come back? Was it to warn me or try to save me?' His voice had turned sharp. 'Or just to satisfy your curiosity? To see the doomed Victorian doctor up close before he expires on schedule?'

'To help, if I can. I'm a nurse so I can't just let you die when I know it's happening and might be able to prevent it.'

'Prevent it.' James laughed bitterly. 'And how exactly do you propose to do that? Tell me to eat more vegetables and get eight hours of sleep? Give me some miraculous future medicine that will cure exhaustion and grief?'

'If necessary, yes. There are treatments and interventions but mostly, you need to stop working yourself into the ground. Rest, eat properly and take care of yourself. None of that is miraculous future medicine, its advice that survived through the ages, because it works.'

'I've heard this lecture before. From Henderson, from

Mrs Barker, from half the town. Everyone has an opinion about what I should do. As if my work could simply stop because I need rest. As if my patients could wait while I take a holiday.'

'Your patients will get another doctor if you die. You, however, will be permanently dead. Which outcome seems preferable?' Lucy realised she was echoing Henderson's words from earlier. 'Sorry. That was harsh, but it's true. If you die on Christmas Day, Dr William Fletcher will arrive in January and take over your practice. I looked it up, your patients will be fine and move on, but you won't.'

James stared at her. 'Dr Fletcher. William Fletcher?'

'You know him?'

'He trained with me in Edinburgh. He's a good doctor. Very competent.' James's voice had gone flat again. 'So, history has it all planned out, does it? I die on schedule, Fletcher takes over, life continues without me. Everything neat and tidy.'

'That's what the records say. But James, I don't think history is as fixed as we assume. The passage exists. Time travel is real and maybe that means things can change so that you don't have to die on Christmas Day.'

'And maybe the passage exists to show me my fate. A cruel joke to say: "Here, have a glimpse of the future, just long enough to learn exactly when you'll die. Merry Christmas."' He stood abruptly and walked to the window, staring out at the gaslit street. 'I can feel it, actually. The exhaustion and the way my heart races. Henderson examined me today. He said I was heading for collapse that my heart would give out if I didn't slow down.'

'Then slow down.'

'I can't. There is a fever outbreak and people are dying. The Dawson boy is eight years old, and his temperature was 105 this morning. Mrs Smith is due to give birth any day, and her last two babies died in childbirth. The Miller family all have scarlet fever, and the youngest is only three. If I rest, they die. If I keep working, I die. Those are my options.'

'What about the other option? Let me help.'

James turned to face her. 'You're from the future. What do you know about Victorian medicine?'

'More than you might think, I've studied medical history. I know about germ theory, antisepsis, the importance of hygiene and what treatments work and those treatments that won't. I can't prescribe or perform surgery, but I can assist, monitor patients, recognise symptoms, provide supportive care. I'm a nurse, James. It's what I'm trained for.'

'A nurse from 2025. With knowledge from the future. Helping me treat patients in 1885.' He almost smiled. 'That's either brilliant or complete insanity.'

'Probably both. But it might keep you alive past Christmas.'

'And if I refuse? If I tell you to go back to your time and leave me to my fate?'

'Then I'll respect that. It's your life and your choice.' Lucy stood and crossed to stand beside him at the window. 'But I hope you won't. Not because I think I can save you, necessarily. But because you deserve a chance and dying at thirty-five from exhaustion and grief is a waste. The world needs good doctors, and you're clearly one of them.'

James was quiet for a long moment, looking out at the street. Then he said: 'You said your device, that telephone thing, contains all human knowledge?'

'Most of it, yes. Through the internet. A global network of connected computers.'

'Could it tell me about medical advances? Things discovered after my time. Treatments for the illnesses I'm currently failing to cure?'

'Yes. Antibiotics, vaccines, modern surgical techniques. All of it.'

'Show me.' He turned to face her, and there was something fierce in his expression now. 'If I'm going to die in two weeks, I want to see it. I want to know what's possible. What medicine becomes and then, I want to see your time. Your 2025. If I'm doomed to die on Christmas Day 1885, I'd like to see the future first.'

'The passage works both ways. You can cross to my time.'

'Then let's do it. Before I lose my nerve and convince myself that this is all stress-induced and send for the asylum wagon.' He picked up her phone from the desk and held it out to her. 'Show me everything. Tell me everything and take me to your world. If I have two weeks left, I don't want to spend them wondering what might have been.'

Lucy took the phone and held out her other hand. 'It's going to be overwhelming. Fair warning. One hundred and forty years of change hits hard.'

'I'm a doctor. I've seen hard things.' His hand closed around hers, warm and solid. 'Besides, what's the worst that could happen? I collapse from shock and die two weeks early? At least I'll have seen something extraordinary first.'

'That's a terrible attitude for a medical professional.'

'Says the woman who travelled through time to warn a stranger about his impending death.'

Lucy smiled despite herself. 'Come on. Let's show you the future. Please try not to have a heart attack when you see central heating.'

'Central what?'

'Heating. It makes a whole house warm all the time without fires.'

'That's impossible.'

'Everything I've shown you tonight is impossible and yet here we are.' She led him toward the passage door. 'My library is much dustier than yours, colder and generally more depressing. I only moved in yesterday, the electricity, and heating will hopefully be working soon, I need to check the app.'

'The app? Electricity in the house? James shook his head. 'I'm following a woman from the future through a secret passage to see an impossible world I can't begin to imagine. If this is madness, it's remarkably detailed madness.'

'It's not madness. Just very, very strange.' Lucy opened the passage door. The darkness stretched ahead. 'Ready?'

'No. But then, I don't think there's any way to be ready for this.' He looked back at his library one last time. The gaslight, the fire in the grate, the papers on his desk. His whole world, familiar and safe. Then he turned to Lucy and nodded. 'All right. Show me the future. Show me your 2025 and what the world becomes.'

'Just remember to breathe. I don't want you to faint when you see modern technology for the first time.'

'I'm a gentleman and I'm a doctor. I do not faint.'

'We'll see.' Lucy stepped into the passage, still holding his hand. 'Come on. Mind your head. The ceiling's low in places.'

The passage was dark, but her phone torch lit the way. Behind her, James followed, his breathing slightly uneven. Whether from anticipation or fear, she couldn't tell.

At the far door, Lucy paused. 'Last chance to change your mind. Once you see it, you can't unsee it. Your world will never look quite the same afterwards.'

'I'm dying in two weeks, Lucy. My world is already changed.' His grip on her hand tightened. 'Open the door. Please.'

So, she did.

They stepped through together into Lucy's cold, dusty library. The contrast was immediate. Grey afternoon light instead of warm gaslight. Dust instead of polish. Silence instead of the crackle of fire.

James stood very still, taking it in. Then he saw the electric light switch on the wall. Walked to it slowly. Touched it with one finger.

'What does this do?'

'It controls the electric light. Try it; it may be connected by now. James pressed the switch and stumbled backwards as soft white light filled the room. 'Is there electric is your room? In your ceiling?' he asked, shielding his eyes, squinting at the bulb. 'Where is the flame?'

'It's a bulb, no fire. It uses very little power and lasts for years. These are everywhere in 2025.'

'Everywhere. Of course.' He sounded faint. 'What else should I brace myself for?'

'Pretty much everything.' Lucy smiled at his expression. 'Come on. Let me show you the modern world. Starting with the kitchen. You're going to love the refrigerator and microwave.'

'I don't know what either of those things are.'

'Exactly. That's the fun part.' She led him toward the door. 'Just try not to break your brain in the first five minutes. We've got a lot to cover.'

James followed her out of the library, his eyes wide, his hand still gripping hers like a lifeline. Behind them, the passage stood open in the bookcase, connecting two worlds and two times with two impossible moments that should never have met.

But they had met, and nothing would be the same again for either of them.

FISH OUT OF WATER

James kept stopping to stare at things on the way to the kitchen. The light switch in the hallway. Then the radiator attached to the wall.

'What's this?' He crouched beside the radiator, holding his hand near it cautiously.

'Central heating. There's a boiler somewhere in the house that heats water, and the hot water circulates through these radiators in pipes throughout the building. The whole house stays warm. No need for fires in every room.'

James stood slowly. 'The whole house, warm. All the time.'

'Well, when it's working. Mine isn't turned on yet because I only moved in yesterday and haven't sorted it out. But normally, yes. You set a thermostat to the temperature you want, and the system maintains it automatically.'

'Automatically.' He touched the radiator again, his medical training overriding fear. Testing temperature, checking for danger. 'This is extraordinary. The fuel costs must be astronomical.'

'Not really. It is cheaper than heating every room individually, actually and much more efficient. Come on. I'll show you the bathroom on the way.'

The bathroom proved even more overwhelming. James stood in the doorway, staring at the white porcelain toilet, the sink with chrome taps and the shower cubicle with its glass door.

'That's a bathtub,' he said, pointing at the shower. 'Except it is vertical and made of glass.'

'It's a shower. You stand in it and water sprays down from above. It washes you much faster than a bath.' Lucy turned it on. Water gushed out immediately, pressurised but cold. 'Hot water normally comes out on demand. There's no need to heat it on a stove or carry it upstairs. It just comes out.'

James reached out and let the water run over his hand. His expression shifted from shock to something like wonder. 'So, this gives you hot water, instantly. In an upstairs room.'

'Normally, yes. All down to plumbing, a water heater and modern engineering.' She turned off the tap. 'The really controversial bit is the toilet. We, uh, we flush waste into the sewer system using clean water. I know, I know. Wasteful and bizarre. But it's sanitary, and the waste goes to treatment plants where it's processed before being released.'

'You defecate into clean drinking water.' James stared at the toilet. 'That's the most barbaric thing I've ever heard.'

'Says the man from an era that dumped chamber pots into the street.'

'We don't... all right, yes, some people do. But using clean water seems obscene when so many don't have access to safe drinking water at all.'

'Fair point and in 2025, we're still working on that problem, honestly. Clean water access isn't universal even now.' Lucy gestured at the shower. 'Want to try it? The shower, I mean. It's quite remarkable.'

'I'm not getting into a vertical bathtub in a house from the future.'

'Your loss. It's one of the best inventions of modern civilisation.' She led him back downstairs. 'Let me show you the kitchen. That's where things get really interesting.'

Interesting turned out to be an understatement. James stood in the kitchen doorway, transfixed by the refrigerator. Lucy opened it to show him the light inside, the cold air, the shelves.

'It's an ice box,' he said. 'Except there's no ice and it's cold all the time. How?'

'Refrigeration. Mechanical process using compressed gas and heat exchange. Honestly, I don't understand the mechanics fully, but it keeps food fresh for weeks. No more needing daily deliveries from the market. You can store milk, meat, vegetables, everything.'

James stepped closer, peering inside at the nearly empty shelves. A carton of milk from Rachel's, some butter, a lonely apple. 'The medical implications are staggering. Food safety, nutrition, disease prevention. How many illnesses could we prevent if we could preserve food like this?'

'Quite a few. Refrigeration revolutionised food safety.' Lucy closed the fridge and turned to the microwave. 'This, however, is pure magic as far as you're concerned. It heats food using electromagnetic radiation. Microwaves. Makes things hot in minutes.'

'Electromagnetic what?'

'Don't worry about it. Just watch.' She put a cup of water in the microwave and set it for one minute. The machine hummed to life, and the turntable rotated while James watched, mesmerised, as the water heated.

When the timer beeped, he jumped. 'It's making noise!'

'That's just to tell you it's done.' Lucy removed the cup and held it up. Steam rose from the surface. 'Boiling water in sixty seconds. No kettle or stove needed. Just electromagnetic radiation exciting the water molecules until they heat up.'

James took the cup from her, testing the temperature carefully with one finger. 'This is witchcraft. I'm watching witchcraft.'

'It's science. Advanced science that would seem like magic to someone from 1885, but it's all based on principles that were being discovered in your time. Maxwell's equations, electromagnetic theory. You're living through the foundations of all this.'

'Maxwell's equations don't explain boxes that heat water by humming at it.'

'Actually, they do. Eventually.' Lucy grinned at his expression. 'Come on. Let me make lunch. You need to eat something. When did you last have a proper meal?'

'Yesterday. I think. Perhaps the day before.' James set the cup down. 'I forget when I'm working.'

'You forget to eat. Excellent medical practice, that. Very professional.' She started assembling sandwiches, pulling bread and cheese from the fridge. 'Sit down before you fall down, you look exhausted.'

'I am exhausted but also exhilarated.' James sat at the kitchen table, watching her work. 'This is extraordinary. All of it. The lights, the heating, the devices. It's like living in a Jules Verne novel.'

'Who?'

'French author. Writes scientific romances and wonderful adventures set in impossible futures with incredible machines.' He paused. 'I suppose his futures aren't that impossible after all, are they?'

'Eat. Doctor's orders.'

'You're not a doctor.'

'Nurse's orders, then. Which are more important because

we're the ones who actually make sure patients do what they're told.'

James took a bite, chewing slowly. After a moment, he said: 'This bread is very soft.'

'Supermarket bread. Mass-produced, pre-sliced, fortified with vitamins. Not as good as proper bakery bread, but convenient.' She made herself a sandwich and sat across from him. 'In my time, you can buy pretty much any food you want at any time of year. Strawberries in winter, oranges all year round, meat from anywhere in the world. Global supply chains. Refrigerated shipping. It's normal.'

'Strawberries in winter,' James said quietly. 'Fresh fruit all year. The scurvy cases alone... children die of malnutrition in my time because they can't access proper food and here, you're telling me it's just available all of the time.'

'For people who can afford it, yes. Poverty and hunger still exist but the potential is there. The technology exists to feed everyone. We just don't always use it well.'

'That's maddeningly frustrating.'

'Welcome to the future. Amazing technology, questionable implementation.' Lucy took a bite of her sandwich. 'After lunch, I'll show you more. The television and computer. Maybe I'll take you outside to see cars properly.'

'Cars?'

'Horseless carriages. Personal vehicles. Nearly everyone has one. They run on petrol, which is refined from oil. Some are electric now, battery powered. They go very fast and make a lot of noise.'

James finished his sandwich in silence. When he spoke again, his voice was thoughtful. 'I've spent years trying to save lives with inadequate tools. Bleeding patients because we don't know what else to do. Watching children die of diseases we can't cure. Losing mothers in childbirth because we don't understand infection. And all the while, in the future, all of these problems are solved. Or at least solvable. It's...'

'Frustrating?'

'Heartbreaking.' He stood and walked to the window. 'What's that?'

Lucy joined him. Outside, a car was pulling into a driveway across the street. 'That's a car like I mentioned, an automobile. Four-wheeled vehicle with an internal combustion engine. Well, that one might be hybrid. It's hard to tell from here.'

James watched the car park, and the driver get out, the doors lock with a chirp and flash of lights. 'That's a horseless carriage. An actual horseless carriage. They're real.'

'Very real.'

'How fast do they go?'

'This street probably has a speed limit of thirty miles per hour. Motorways, which are large roads connecting cities, allow seventy. Some cars can go much faster, though that's illegal on public roads.'

'Seventy miles per hour.' James sat down on the arm of the sofa, his eyes never leaving the window. 'A human being, travelling at seventy miles per hour, in a machine.'

'We can go faster in the air.'

'I'm sorry, what?'

'Aeroplanes. Aircraft. We fly now and have done for over a century. Powered flight was achieved in 1903, just eighteen years after your time. Now we have commercial airlines that can take you anywhere in the world in hours. London to New York in seven hours. London to Australia in about twenty.'

James's face had gone very pale. 'Humans can fly; you're telling me that humans can fly.'

'In aeroplanes, yes which are basically big metal tubes with wings and engines. Jet engines now, mostly. They're very safe, statistically safer than cars.' Lucy paused. 'Are you all right? You look like you might faint.'

'I don't faint; I told you that.' But he did put his head between his knees for a moment. When he straightened, he said: 'Seventy miles per hour on the ground. Crossing oceans in hours through the air. What else? What other impossible things are normal in your time?'

'Space travel. We've been to the moon, sent robots to Mars, have satellites orbiting Earth that handle communication and navigation. The internet, which I mentioned earlier. Global instantaneous communication. You can talk to someone on the other side of the world in real time, see their face, share information. Medical imaging that lets us see inside the body without cutting it open. There are organ transplants, genetic engineering, and artificial intelligence.'

'Stop. Please stop.' James held up a hand. 'My brain is going to explode. That's too much impossible news for one afternoon.'

'Sorry. I got carried away.' Lucy smiled apologetically. 'How about I show you the television instead? That's just moving pictures with sound. Much less conceptually challenging than space travel.'

The television proved both fascinating and disturbing. James watched a nature documentary about lions for ten minutes in complete silence. When Lucy changed the channel to a cooking show, he stood up abruptly.

'There are people inside that box.'

'No, they're images. Recorded earlier and broadcast through the air to receivers in people's homes. The television picks up the signal and displays it.'

'People are inside the box.' He repeated, waving his hand in front of their faces, 'can they see me?'

'No, and they are not actually inside, it's just their image, a little like a photograph, but moving. Like the video I showed you on my phone, but bigger.' Lucy turned it off. 'Maybe that's enough for now. You're looking a bit overwhelmed.'

'Overwhelmed doesn't begin to cover it.' James walked back to the window. Outside, another car passed. A plane flew overhead, leaving a white contrail across the grey sky. He pointed at it. 'What in God's name is that?'

'Aeroplane with humans flying in it.'

'Of course. Humans flying. Why not?' His voice had gone slightly hysterical. 'Humans flying through the sky in metal tubes at impossible speeds. Obviously.'

'James, sit down. You're going to make yourself ill.'

'I'm already ill. I'm dying in two weeks, remember? Might as well have my brain broken by the future before my heart gives out.'

'That's a terrible attitude.'

'Says the woman showing me witchcraft boxes and flying machines.' But he did sit down heavily on the sofa. 'This is too much. All of it. The technology alone is staggering, but the implications... Lucy, do you understand what this means for medicine? For treating patients?'

'I have some idea, yes.'

'Show me. Please, I need to see what medicine becomes. If I'm going to die in two weeks, I want to know what was possible. What I would have seen if I'd lived.'

Lucy hesitated, then nodded. She got her laptop from the library and opened it on the coffee table. The screen glowed to life. James leaned forward, transfixed.

'Another glowing box.'

'It's a computer. Sort of a very advanced mechanical calculator combined with a typewriter and a library. This is how we access the internet. Watch.' She opened a browser and searched for 'history of antibiotics.' Articles appeared. Images of Alexander Fleming and his petri dishes. Explanations of penicillin, how it worked, what it cured.

James read in silence. His hands trembled slightly as they scrolled through the articles, Lucy guiding him on how to use the trackpad.

'Antibiotics,' he whispered. 'Drugs that kill bacteria. Actually, kill it. Infections that are fatal in my time are cured with pills. Simple pills.'

'Fleming discovered penicillin in 1928. By the 1940s, it was being mass-produced and saved millions of lives. Hundreds of millions, probably. They changed everything.'

'Show me more.'

Lucy searched for vaccines. Showed him the history of immunisation. Polio, smallpox, measles, diphtheria. Diseases that killed or crippled thousands are now preventable with simple injections.

When they reached Diphtheria, James stopped her. 'Wait. Go back to the diphtheria vaccine.'

She clicked back to the article. James read it slowly, his eyes moving over every word. Information about the vaccine's development, its efficacy, and the lives saved. When he finished, he sat back, his face wet with tears.

'The children,' he said, his voice breaking. 'All the children I've lost to diphtheria who were choking and unable to breathe. Dying in front of me while I stood there helpless and it's preventable. A simple vaccine.'

Lucy closed the laptop gently. 'You couldn't have known, the vaccine didn't exist in your time. You did everything possible with the tools you had.'

'But now I do know and I have to go back to a time where I can't save them. Where I must watch children die of diseases that are completely preventable in your world. How do I do that? How do I go back and face my patients knowing what I know now?'

'The same way that in my time face patients with diseases we can't cure yet. We all do our best and provide what comfort we can. We don't give up just because we can't fix everything.' Lucy moved to sit beside him on the sofa. 'James, you're a good doctor, that's obvious. But you can't save everyone. No one can. Not in 1885, not in 2025. We're all limited by what's possible in our time.'

'It's not enough.'

'It never feels like enough. That's what makes you a good doctor rather than a mediocre one. The good ones always feel like they should do more.'

James wiped his eyes roughly. 'I'm sorry, this is completely unprofessional. Crying over vaccines that don't exist yet.'

'You're allowed to grieve for your patients, and for what's not possible. That's not unprofessional. That's human.' She paused, then added: 'You need to go back, though, your patients need you, and you've been gone for hours. Mrs Barker will be frantic. But James, promise me you'll take care of yourself. Eat and sleep or you won't make it past Christmas.'

'Why do you care?' He turned to look at her, his eyes red. 'You barely know me. Why does it matter to you whether I live or die?'

'Because I just care, I care about people. I guess it's why I became a nurse, I felt it's where I belonged, in a place where I could save people, it's what I do. Or what I did, before I was made redundant.' Lucy found herself speaking without quite meaning to. 'And because I see myself in you, if I'm honest. The self-destruction, working too hard, caring too much, letting it consume you until there's nothing left. I did that. After my divorce, after everything fell apart. I worked myself into exhaustion thinking if I was useful enough, competent enough, I'd matter and be worth something.'

'Divorce!' he blanched. 'You are a divorced lady?'

'Let's get some perspective here, James. Divorce is common some people have three, four marriages, more sometimes and then get divorced and start again.'

James stared at her speculatively. Deciding to move on. 'Did it work?'

'What? Divorce?'

'No, working yourself to exhaustion to help you to move on.'

'No, I got made redundant anyway. It was all budget cuts, nothing personal. Turns out working yourself to death doesn't guarantee job security.' She laughed, but it came out bitter. 'So yes, I care because I understand. This feeling of emptiness and the sense that work is the only thing holding you together, and if you stop, you'll shatter completely.'

James was quiet for a moment. Then he said: 'You understand.'

'Yes.'

'After Eleanor died, medicine was all I had left. The only thing that made sense and the only way to feel like I was worth something. I was saving others because I couldn't save her.'

'I know that feeling. I do.'

'Then we're both a mess.' He almost smiled. 'How reassuring.'

'Apparently. Two people falling apart, shown to each other across time. Maybe that's why the passage exists. As a warning. Look, here's someone making the same mistakes you are, so do better.'

'Or as a chance to do better,' Lucy said quietly. 'Maybe we're not meant to be warnings. Maybe we're meant to help each other. You remind me why I became a nurse and why I loved it. After the redundancy, I thought I'd failed. That I wasn't good enough, but talking to you, seeing your dedication, it reminds me that the work matters. Even when it's hard and especially when we can't save everyone.'

'You're an optimist.'

'Sometimes.' She stood and held out her hand. 'Come on. I'll walk you back through the passage. You need to eat something proper, sleep in your own bed, check on your patients and I need to think about what I'm doing. Whether I can actually help or if I'm just making things worse.'

James took her hand and stood. 'You're not making things worse. You are making my circumstances strange, impossible, and occasionally terrifying, yes. But not worse.' He looked around the room one last time. The electric lights, the laptop, the television. All the impossible things that were normal in 2025. 'Thank you for showing me this, trusting me with it and caring whether I live or die.'

'Thank you for believing me. For not having me committed to an asylum.'

'The day's not over yet. I may still have myself committed.' But he smiled as he said it. 'How do I turn off this electric light? I should learn that, shouldn't I, if I'm going to keep visiting, if I am allowed to visit again?'

'Of course, you can and the light, you just flip the switch. Like this.' Lucy demonstrated. On. Off. On. Off.

'Remarkable. Absurdly simple once you know how.' James practiced a few times, clearly delighted despite his exhaustion. 'In my time, this would be considered miraculous. Magic beyond imagining and here it's so ordinary you don't even think about it.'

'Everything extraordinary becomes ordinary eventually.' She led him back to the library and the passage door. 'Same time tomorrow? I can help with your patients if you'll let me. Between the two of us, we might keep your workload manageable.'

'A nurse from the future helping me treat Victorian patients. What could possibly go wrong?' But his eyes were warm. 'All right. Tomorrow at the same time.'

'I'll bring medical knowledge and hopefully try to dig out some common sense.' Lucy opened the passage door. 'Go on. Mrs Barker is probably sending out search parties.'

James stepped into the passage, then turned back. 'Lucy?'

'Yes?'

'I'm glad the passage brought us together. Whatever the reason and whatever happens.' He smiled, tired but genuine. 'Thank you.'

'Thank you for giving me something to care about again. I'd forgotten what that felt like.'

'Then we're even.' He disappeared into the darkness of the passage.

Lucy stood in the doorway for a moment, listening to his footsteps fade. Then she closed the door and the bookcase, sealing off 1885 once more.

The library felt very empty without him. Quiet and cold. Just a dusty room in a neglected house, waiting for something to change. But perhaps something already had.

Lucy turned off the overhead light and stood in the growing darkness, thinking about time and connection and two broken people trying to save each other across 140 years.

Perhaps the passage had brought them together for a reason, and maybe they really could help each other. Perhaps some things were worth hoping for, even when hope seemed impossible.

Outside in Otley, cars passed, aeroplanes flew overhead and life continued in 2025, ordinary and extraordinary all at once.

And in 1885, a Victorian doctor walked back to his gaslit

world, carrying knowledge of futures he'd never see and hope he thought he'd lost.

Two times. Two people. One impossible connection.

THE ROUTINE

Over the next few days, they established a pattern. Lucy would cross through in the mornings, spending time in 1885 helping James with his rounds. Evenings brought James to 2025, where he learned about the modern world with the enthusiasm of a child with the analytical mind of a scientist.

On the third morning, Lucy arrived to find Mrs Barker in the library, dusting the bookshelves with fierce concentration. The housekeeper turned at the sound of the passage door opening, her eyes narrowing.

'You're the strange woman,' Mrs Barker said flatly. 'The one who appeared from nowhere. Dr Ashworth said you'd be coming.'

'Lucy Patterson.' She held out her hand and then dropped it awkwardly when it was refused. 'I'm here to help with the patients, if that's all right.'

Mrs Barker's gaze travelled down Lucy's jeans and jumper with obvious disapproval. 'What kind of woman wears trousers?'

'The practical kind. They are much easier for moving

around in, bending down and for doing work in.' Lucy decided directness was probably best. 'I know this is strange and that my clothes are odd. But I promise I'm here to help, not cause trouble. James is working himself to death, and I have medical training that might be useful.'

'Medical training.' The housekeeper's tone suggested profound scepticism. 'In what, exactly?'

'Nursing. Twelve years' experience. I know anatomy, physiology, disease processes, patient care. I can monitor symptoms, provide treatments, recognise when someone's deteriorating.' She met Mrs Barker's eyes steadily. 'Dr Ashworth needs help; you know that as you've been trying to get him to slow down for months, he told me. Maybe I can take some of the burden.'

Something in Mrs Barker's expression shifted. Not quite trust, but perhaps the beginning of it. 'He does need help, he works himself to the bone, that man and hasn't had a proper night's sleep since Mrs Ashworth passed, God rest her. The man won't eat unless I practically force food down his throat.'

'Then let me help. Please.'

Mrs Barker studied her for a long moment. Then she nodded sharply. 'All right. But if you cause him any trouble, any trouble at all, I'll box your ears myself. I don't care what strange place you come from or what odd clothes you wear. Understood?'

'Understood.' Lucy smiled despite herself. 'Thank you.'

'Don't thank me yet. There are three house calls this morning, starting with the Dawson boy. That fever still hasn't broken, and Dr Ashworth is worried about him.' Here is the address with directions. She passed Lucy a piece of paper with James's neat handwriting on it.

The Dawson house was small, cramped and bitterly cold. Six children shared two beds in the upstairs room. Young

Timothy lay in the corner bed, his face flushed, his breathing laboured. His mother hovered nearby, wringing her hands, her face grey with exhaustion.

James was bent over the boy, stethoscope pressed to his thin chest. When he saw Lucy, relief flashed across his face.

'Mrs Dawson, this is my new assistant, Miss Patterson. She'll be helping me with Timothy's care.'

Mrs Dawson looked Lucy up and down, taking in the trousers, the modern clothing. But she was too worried about her son to care much. 'Can you help him? Please? He's been like this for days now.'

Lucy moved to the other side of the bed, looking at the boy properly. Seven years old, James had said. Fever, laboured breathing, chest infection. In 2025, this would be antibiotics and fluids. In 1885, it was supportive care and hope.

'May I examine him?' Lucy asked James quietly.

'Please do.'

She checked Timothy's pulse; it was fast and thready. His skin was hot and dry under her fingers. Pupils equal and reactive when she lifted his eyelids. Breathing was rapid and shallow, all the classic signs of severe infection and dehydration.

'He needs fluids,' Lucy said. 'Cool compresses to bring the fever down. We should open the windows, get fresh air circulating and he needs to be sitting up more. That angle isn't helping his breathing.'

James nodded. 'Mrs Dawson, can you fetch clean water and cloths? We'll need several changes and open that window, please. I know it's cold, but the fresh air will help.'

'Open the window? But he'll catch his death...'

'Fresh air won't harm him, but stale air might.' Lucy spoke gently but firmly. 'In modern medicine, we know that ventilation is crucial for respiratory infections. The fresh air will help him breathe better.'

Mrs Dawson looked uncertain, but she moved to open the window. The cold December air flooded in. The other children huddled under their blankets, but Timothy's breathing eased slightly almost immediately.

Together, Lucy and James worked. Cool compresses on the boy's forehead and wrists. Small sips of water administered slowly. Adjusting his position to help his lungs expand more easily. It was basic nursing care but done with knowledge and precision.

After an hour, Timothy's fever had dropped slightly, and his breathing was easier. Not cured, not by a long shot, but stabilised.

'Keep doing this,' James told Mrs Dawson. 'A cool compress every hour. Fresh water to drink whenever he'll take it. If he worsens, send for me immediately. But I think he's turned a corner.'

Outside, walking to their next call, James said quietly: 'That was excellent work. The way you assessed him, prioritised the interventions. Where did you learn that?'

'Hospital nursing. You learn to triage quickly, focus on what matters most. ABC, we call it. Airway, breathing, circulation and then everything else comes after.' Lucy pulled her coat tighter against the cold. 'He'll recover, I think, as long as he stays hydrated and the fever breaks.'

'In your time, you'd give him antibiotics.'

'Yes, for him we would. Though we're more cautious with them now as antibiotic resistance is becoming a problem. We've overused them, and bacteria are evolving to resist them.' She glanced at him. 'How are you feeling? Did you eat breakfast?'

'Yes, mother hen. Mrs Barker made me porridge and watched while I ate every bite.'

'Good. Keep that up.'

Their next patient was Mr Harrison, a man in his fifties with what James diagnosed as rheumatic fever. Lucy helped change his dressings, noting the inflammation in his joints with clinical interest. In 2025, this would be controlled with anti-inflammatory drugs. In 1885, it was rest, cooling measures, and hope the heart wasn't too damaged.

By midday, they'd seen five patients. Lucy was exhausted, but James looked energised. Working together seemed to lighten his burden and make the impossible caseload more manageable.

At the final house, was an elderly woman with pneumonia, one of the neighbours stopped them on the way out.

'Dr Ashworth you have a new assistant, I see. Strange woman, wearing trousers.'

'Miss Patterson is very competent,' James said firmly. 'I'm fortunate to have her help.'

The neighbour peered at Lucy with undisguised curiosity. 'Where are you from, miss? You don't sound local.'

'Leeds,' Lucy said, which was technically true. 'I trained at the hospital there.'

'Leeds. Modern ideas in the cities, I suppose. Still, if Dr Ashworth vouches for you, that's good enough for me.' The woman nodded and went back inside.

Walking back to James's house, Lucy said: 'That went better than expected. I thought they'd be more scandalised by the trousers.'

'They're more concerned about their health than your clothing. Besides, you're helping me save lives and that earns you considerable goodwill.' James smiled at her. 'Though I imagine the gossip will be extraordinary. "Dr Ashworth's peculiar new assistant who wears men's clothing and speaks with strange authority." I'll be the talk of Otley within days.'

'Sorry about that.'

'Don't be. I haven't cared what people think for quite some time.' He paused at his front door. 'Will you come in? Mrs Barker always makes too much food for lunch. You should eat something before going back.'

'I should get back. Let you rest before evening surgery hours.'

'Lucy, you've been working all morning. You need to eat too. Physician, heal thyself, and all that.' When she hesitated, he added: 'Please? I'd like the company. Mrs Barker is wonderful, but she tends to lecture rather than converse.'

'All right. But only if you promise to rest this afternoon. No sneaking out to see extra patients.'

'I promise.'

He opened the door. 'Come on. Let's see what culinary delight Mrs Barker has prepared.'

Lunch was stew, thick and hearty, served in the warm kitchen. Mrs Barker bustled about, clearly pleased to have people to feed. She'd warmed to Lucy considerably after hearing about her work with patients.

'You know your medicine, I'll give you that,' the housekeeper said, ladling stew into bowls. 'And you got Dr Ashworth to eat without me having to threaten him. That's worth its weight in gold.'

'Happy to help,' Lucy said. 'He does need to eat more, though and sleep. When was the last time you had a full night's rest?' Lucy directed her question at James.

'Define full night.'

'Eight hours of uninterrupted sleep.'

'Then the answer is not in recent memory. I get called out most nights. Emergencies don't keep convenient hours.'

'What if we set up a system? I could take some of the night calls. Do the basic assessments, stabilise patients until morning and call on you only if it's genuinely urgent.'

James shook his head. 'I can't ask you to do that.'

'You're not asking. I'm offering. I can't perform surgery, but I can assess, monitor, provide initial care. It would give you a chance to sleep through the night occasionally. Which you desperately need.'

Mrs Barker set down her ladle with a decisive thunk. 'She's right, Dr Ashworth. You need proper rest, let the girl help. The Lord knows you need it.'

'The girl has a name,' Lucy said mildly. 'But yes, please let me help. You're no good to your patients if you collapse from exhaustion.'

James looked between them, outnumbered. Finally, he sighed. 'All right. But only for the next week. After that... well, we'll see.'

After that, he'd be dead. But neither of them said it.

That evening, James crossed through to 2025. Lucy had spent the afternoon cleaning the kitchen properly and shopping for groceries. When he emerged from the passage, she was cooking pasta, a skill she'd learned at university and mostly forgotten until now.

'What's that smell?' James appeared in the kitchen doorway, sniffing appreciatively. 'It's extraordinary.'

'Tomato sauce with garlic, basil, olive oil. Nothing fancy, but it's hot and filling.' She gestured at the kitchen table, now clean and set with two plates. 'Sit. You're eating a proper meal tonight whether you like it or not.'

'I'm starting to see why Mrs Barker likes you. You both have the same autocratic approach to feeding people.' But he sat obediently. 'What's this called?'

'Spaghetti Bolognese. Well, a simple version. Originally Italian food and very popular here.' She served him a generous portion. 'Eat and then we'll work on your education about the modern world. I thought tonight we could tackle the internet properly.'

The internet fascinated and horrified James in equal

measure. Sitting at Lucy's laptop, he searched for medical journals, historical records, information about diseases he was currently treating. Within an hour, he'd absorbed information that would have taken weeks of library research to acquire in 1885.

'This is staggering,' he said, scrolling through an article about pneumonia treatment. 'Instant access to the latest medical research. Case studies from around the world. Lucy, do you understand how revolutionary this is?'

'I take it for granted, honestly, everyone in my time does. If you don't know something, you just look it up online. It's normal.'

'Normal. The sum of human knowledge available in seconds, and it's normal.' He shook his head. 'What I could do with this in my time. Just to think of the lives I could save.'

'You're saving lives now. With the tools you have, that's what matters.' Lucy sat beside him, showing him how to navigate between pages, how to use search engines effectively. 'Besides, even with all this information, medicine in my time isn't perfect. We still lose patients and face diseases we can't cure. Cancer, degenerative conditions, complex chronic illnesses. The tools get better, but the struggle continues.'

'That's oddly comforting. Not that people still die, but that doctors still fight and still try.' He looked at her. 'You miss it, don't you? Nursing. The work.'

'Yes. More than I realised.' Lucy closed the laptop. 'After the redundancy, I told myself it was just a job. That I could do something else. But working with you these past few days, helping with patients... I'd forgotten how much I loved it. The challenge, the purpose. Making a real difference in people's lives.'

'You're making a difference in mine,' James said quietly. 'These past few days, having someone to share the burden...

I'd forgotten what that felt like. I was working with Eleanor occasionally, before she died and having a partner, someone who understands eases the burden enormously.'

'Eleanor was a nurse?'

'Not formally. But she helped me every now and again with patients. She was practical, calm, and extraordinarily competent. Much like you, actually.' His expression turned sad. 'She would have liked you and would have appreciated your no-nonsense approach and your questionable clothing choices.'

'My clothing is perfectly sensible, thank you very much.'

'You're wearing trousers. Women don't wear trousers.'

'Women in 2025 wear whatever they like. Trousers, skirts, dresses, shorts. We fought for that right.' Lucy stood and held out her hand. 'Come on, if you're going to judge my fashion, I should at least show you a proper supermarket, where other women will undoubtedly be wearing trousers, besides, you'll lose your mind over the abundance.'

The supermarket was a ten-minute walk down the hill. James stared at the automatic doors, which slid open as they approached.

'Doors that open themselves. Of course they do. Why wouldn't doors open themselves in the future?' But his voice held wonder as well as sarcasm.

Inside, he stopped dead. Aisle after aisle of food stretched in every direction. Bright lights overhead illuminated everything with harsh clarity. Music played softly from hidden speakers. People pushed trolleys, examined products, and checked prices of competitors' identical products on their phones.

'This is...' James walked slowly down the first aisle, his eyes trying to take in everything at once. 'How much food is here?'

'Thousands of products and this is just a medium-sized

supermarket. There are bigger ones.' Lucy grabbed a basket. 'Come on, I need milk and bread, and you can explore.'

Exploring took longer than expected. James stopped at every display, reading labels, examining packaging, asking endless questions. In the produce section, he picked up a pineapple and stared at it in disbelief.

'These are from the tropics. They cost a fortune to import and here it's just sitting in a pile, available to anyone.'

'Global shipping in refrigerated containers. We can get fresh produce from anywhere in the world within days.' Lucy selected apples, dropping them into the basket. 'Most people don't think about it and just buy what they fancy for dinner.'

The frozen food section fascinated him even more. He opened one of the freezer doors and stood in the blast of cold air, peering at the rows of frozen meals.

'These are complete dinners. You just heat them and eat them?'

'Microwave meals. They are very convenient but not particularly nutritious, very popular with people who work long hours.' She steered him away before he could read every single label. 'Come on. The pharmacy section is more impressive.'

The pharmacy area nearly made him weep. Row after row of over-the-counter medicines. Pain relief, fever reducers, cold remedies, antihistamines, digestive aids. Everything neatly packaged, clearly labelled, readily available.

When he picked up a packet of paracetamol and just stood there holding it, Lucy touched his arm gently.

'What's wrong?'

'Acetaminophen for pain relief and fever reduction and anyone can purchase it. No prescription needed.' His voice was thick. 'Do you know how many patients I see in pain? Children burning with fever? And here it's just... on a shelf. Anyone can buy it.'

'We take it for granted. All of this, the abundance, the access. You're seeing it with fresh eyes, and it's making me realise how extraordinary it really is.'

James replaced the paracetamol carefully and moved to the next aisle. 'These would save thousands in my time. Tens of thousands and here they're just available. Cheap and easy.'

'Modern manufacturing, global supply chains, economies of scale. None of which helps your patients in 1885.'

'No. But knowing it's possible helps me and reminds me why I keep going. Because someday, in the future, medicine will be better. Medicine will be this.' He gestured at the pharmacy shelves. 'Even if I don't live to see it, it's coming and that is what matters.'

They walked home with a carrier bag of groceries. James wanted to carry it, fascinated by the plastic bag itself.

'This material is extraordinary. Waterproof, lightweight, incredibly strong. What's it made from?'

'Plastic. Petroleum-based polymer, very useful, but terrible for the environment. We use too much of it, and it doesn't break down naturally. One of the many problems we haven't solved yet.'

'The future is complicated.'

'Very. We solve some problems and create others.'

Back at the house, they ate ice cream from the freezer. James's reaction to frozen dessert was everything Lucy had hoped for.

'This is impossibly cold yet sweet and creamy. What is this magic?'

'Ice cream. Frozen dairy dessert. It is very popular in summer, but honestly, it's good any time.' Lucy handed him the tub. 'There's more. Here, have as much as you want, you need the calories.'

They sat at the kitchen table, sharing ice cream and talking about medicine, about patients, about the impossible situation they'd found themselves in. Small touches happened naturally now. Lucy's hand on his arm when making a point. His shoulder brushed hers as they leaned over the laptop together. The comfort of two people learning to trust each other.

'Tell me about your redundancy,' James said suddenly. 'You've mentioned it but not really explained what happened.'

Lucy set down her spoon. 'It was down to budget cuts. The NHS is chronically underfunded. They closed an entire ward, made twelve of us redundant. It wasn't personal, they said. Just numbers on a spreadsheet. Twelve nurses who became unemployed in a single meeting.'

'But this NHS, people simply present themselves to a hospital or to a doctor and then they are treated? No one has to pay?'

'Well, sort of, we contribute when we pay tax but no, no one is asked for payment or turned away due to their lack of money.'

'Extraordinary. But this NHS does not have enough money, how can it continue if people such as yourself, good, qualified people are dismissed? That must have been devastating.'

'It was and is. I'd worked on that ward for five years, I knew the consultants, the regular patients, and the rhythm of the place. Then, one day it was just gone. They gave us two months' notice and a redundancy payment that wouldn't cover three months' rent in Leeds.' She took another bite of ice cream. 'The divorce was hard, but I expected that. Marriages fail all the time. But losing my job? I'd thought if I was good enough, worked hard enough, I'd be safe. It turns out I was wrong.'

'You blame yourself.'

'Yes, it's easy to blame ourselves for things that deep-down we know we have no power over. Do you blame yourself for Eleanor's death?'

James was quiet for a moment. 'Yes, every day. She had pneumonia and I treated her, but it wasn't enough. I should have done more, and I certainly should have noticed the symptoms earlier, should have...' He trailed off. 'But she died anyway and I've spent a year punishing myself for not being good enough to save her.'

'We can't save everyone; you told me that yourself.'

'Yes. I understand that too well.'

After James returned to 1885, Lucy sat alone in the kitchen, thinking. Five days until Christmas when James was supposed to die in his surgery, alone and exhausted, his heart giving out after months of self-destruction.

But he was eating now. Sleeping better and sharing the workload and she could see the difference already. The colour was returning to his face, his hands steadier hands and less shadowed eyes. Was it enough? Could they really change history?

Lucy cleared the ice cream bowls and washed them slowly, thinking. Tomorrow she'd talk to James seriously about the future choices and surviving until after Christmas. Because something would have to happen. The calendar was running out.

THE VICTORIAN CHRISTMAS MARKET

*D*ecember 21st dawned bright and cold. Lucy woke to frost patterns on the bedroom window and the distant sound of church bells.

James needed a break from patients and worry. He needed to remember what Christmas could be, what joy looked like, and Otley's Victorian Christmas Market seemed like the perfect opportunity.

When she crossed through to 1885 that morning, she found James already awake, sitting at his desk writing patient notes. Dark circles still shadowed his eyes, but he looked better than a week ago. Less gaunt, more present.

'No patients this morning,' Lucy announced. 'We're taking the day off.'

James looked up, startled. 'I have three house calls scheduled and evening surgery.'

'Mrs Barker can handle messages and surely anyone urgent can wait until this afternoon. You're coming with me to see something special.' She held out her hand. 'Trust me, you need this.'

'Lucy, I can't just abandon my patients…'

'You're not abandoning anyone. You're taking one morning off. When was the last time you did something just for enjoyment?'

James set down his pen slowly. 'I honestly can't remember.'

'Then it's definitely time. Come on, get your coat. Well, not your Victorian coat, you'll need something more modern. I think there's an old jacket of my ex-husbands in the wardrobe that I accidentally packed.'

Twenty minutes later, James stood in Lucy's bedroom wearing jeans, a jumper, and a waterproof jacket. He looked utterly bizarre; a Victorian gentleman dressed in 21st-century casual wear. His hair was still combed in that precise Victorian style, which only added to the oddness of his appearance.

'I feel ridiculous,' he said, pulling at the jeans. 'These are extraordinarily uncomfortable; how do people wear these?'

'You get used to them. Besides, you can't go to a Victorian Christmas market wearing actual Victorian clothes. People would think you were taking the costume element far too seriously.' Lucy handed him a scarf. 'Here, it's cold out.'

'A Victorian Christmas market? In 2025?'

'They are very popular. Vendors dress up in period costume, sell traditional crafts and food, everyone pretends they've travelled back in time. It's quite charming. Though I suspect you'll find it more amusing than charming.'

The market was set up in the town centre, stalls lining the cobbled streets. Fairy lights hung between lampposts, and a large Christmas tree dominated the square. Music played from hidden speakers, a mix of carols and Victorian-era songs. People wandered between stalls wearing modern winter coats, many clutching paper cups of mulled wine.

James stopped at the edge of the market, taking it all in.

His expression shifted from curiosity to fascination to barely suppressed amusement.

'This is meant to be Victorian?' He pointed at a stall where the vendor wore a crinoline dress over jeans and trainers. 'That woman's skirt is historically accurate, but her shoes are visible and completely wrong. No Victorian woman would wear those.'

'It's just for fun. Historical accuracy isn't really the point.'

'Clearly.' He moved closer to a food stall advertising 'Authentic Victorian Chestnuts.' The vendor, a man in his twenties wearing a top hat and waistcoat over a hoodie, was roasting chestnuts over a gas burner. 'Authentic chestnuts roasted over a gas flame. How wonderfully contradictory.'

Lucy bit back a laugh. 'Try not to correct everyone. People are just trying to enjoy themselves.'

'But the historical inaccuracies are extraordinary. Look at that stall selling "Victorian Christmas puddings." But using decorations that are modern plastic.'

'James, you're literally from the Victorian era. Of course it's going to seem inaccurate to you. For everyone else, it's close enough.'

'Close enough,' he muttered, but he was smiling. 'All right, I'll try to restrain my pedantic impulses. Try being the operative word.'

They wandered through the market, James providing a running commentary on every anachronism. The costume stall drew particular scorn.

'Those aren't Victorian dresses. Those are modern interpretations of Victorian fashion. Look at the seams, the fabric, the way they're constructed. No Victorian seamstress would have made something so slovenly.'

'Slovenly? They look fine to me.'

'The stitching is all wrong and that fabric is synthetic. We don't have synthetic fabrics in my time. Everything is natural fibres: cotton, wool, silk, linen.' He picked up a bonnet and examined it critically. 'This is held together with glue. Glue! The ribbon should be sewn on properly.'

'You're being insufferable.'

'I'm being accurate. There's a difference.' But his eyes were bright with amusement. 'I'm sorry. This is just deeply strange. Watching people in my future dress up as people from my present. It's like... I don't know. Like watching a play about your own life where all the actors have got the details wrong.'

At the next stall, a vendor was demonstrating 'authentic Victorian cooking techniques' using an electric hot plate disguised with a decorative cover.

'That's an electric heating element,' James said flatly. 'Disguised under a metal cover to look like a coal range. But you can see the power cord running behind that barrel.'

'James, please. You're going to get us thrown out.'

'I'm simply observing with historically accurate criticism.' He moved closer to watch the vendor making what was advertised as 'Traditional Victorian Gingerbread'. 'Those spices are all wrong and why use self-raising flour?' he asked, looking at the packet. 'We'd use plain flour and add our own raising agents. Bicarbonate of soda, usually. Or eggs beaten until they're foamy.'

The vendor looked up, defensive. 'This is based on historical recipes.'

'Loosely based, perhaps. But the proportions are all wrong there is too much ginger, not enough treacle and you're mixing it far too quickly. Victorian baking requires patience. You should be creaming that butter and sugar for at least ten minutes by hand.'

'Are you a food historian?'

'I'm from 1885,' James said pleasantly. 'So yes, in a manner of speaking.'

Lucy dragged him away before he could elaborate. 'You can't tell people you're from 1885. They'll think you're mad.'

'They'd be right, I am. I'm having a romance with a woman from 140 years in my future. That's the definition of madness.' He caught her expression. 'Sorry. Did I say romance? I meant friendship. Obviously.'

'Obviously,' Lucy echoed, her heart doing something complicated in her chest. 'Come on. Let's find something you can't criticise.'

A stallholder dressed as a Victorian gentleman offered them samples of mince pies. James accepted one, bit into it, and his eyebrows rose.

'That's rather good. The spices are excellent.'

'Told you it wasn't all bad.' Lucy tried her own pie. Warm, sweet, perfectly spiced. 'These are lovely.'

They moved on to a stall selling wooden toys. James picked up a carved horse, examining the craftsmanship with interest.

'This is well-made. Traditional joinery with a proper finish. Someone who knows what they're doing made this.' He set it down carefully. 'In my time, toys like this are common. Every child has something similar. I suppose in your time they're considered quaint.'

'Most children now have electronic toys. Phones, gaming devices, robots. Wooden toys are popular with parents who want something traditional, but they're not the norm.'

'Electronic toys.' James shook his head. 'Of course. Why play with carved horses when you can have glowing rectangles that make noise?'

'You sound like every parent lamenting modern childhood. "In my day we played with sticks and were grateful!"'

'In my day, we did play with sticks. And hoops and occasionally dead rats, which I don't recommend.' He caught her expression and laughed. 'I grew up in Yorkshire. We weren't precious about our play.'

They stopped at a Christmas tree stall, where a heated debate was happening between two vendors about the proper way to decorate a Victorian Christmas tree.

'Candles!' insisted one. 'Real candles, that's how the Victorians did it.'

'LED lights shaped like candles,' the other argued. 'Safer and just as authentic looking.'

James leaned close to Lucy and whispered: 'Neither is correct. Prince Albert popularised Christmas trees in Britain in the 1840s, yes, but they weren't universally adopted until later. Most families in my time don't have trees at all. It's still quite a new tradition.'

'Are you enjoying yourself?' Lucy asked. 'Cataloguing all the historical inaccuracies?'

'Immensely. This is the most entertainment I've had in months.' He smiled at her. It was genuine and warm. 'Thank you for insisting I come. I didn't realise how much I needed this and to not be Dr Ashworth for a few hours and just be James, walking through a market with someone I...' He paused, then finished: 'With a friend.'

'A friend who dragged you into the future and forced you to wear uncomfortable jeans.'

'The best kind of friend, clearly.'

Near the town square, a group of carol singers had gathered. They wore Victorian-style costumes, holding song sheets, harmonising beautifully on 'God Rest Ye Merry Gentlemen'. James stopped to listen, his expression softening.

'This, at least, is accurate. We sing this carol. Exactly this arrangement.' He hummed along quietly, then said: 'Though that woman in the back is a soprano trying to sing alto. She keeps drifting sharp.'

'Can you not? Can you just enjoy the music without analysing it?'

'I'm a doctor, I analyse everything. It's a professional hazard.' But he smiled. 'They're good, though. Better than our church choir, if I'm honest. Mrs Henderson sings like a crow with bronchitis.'

'That's unkind.'

'But accurate. You'd understand if you'd heard her attempt "O Come All Ye Faithful" last Christmas. Several people left early claiming they had a fever. At least these singers are competent. And the tenor has excellent breath control. Probably doesn't smoke.'

'Probably vapes instead.'

'Vapes?'

'Electronic cigarettes. I'll explain later. On second thoughts, I won't. One impossible technology per day is enough.'

They reached a stall selling antique Christmas decorations. Glass baubles hung from ribbons, catching the winter light. Some were new but made to look old. Others were genuinely vintage, price tags reflecting their age and rarity.

James stopped abruptly, staring at one particular bauble. It was glass, hand-painted with delicate red and gold flowers. Victorian, definitely. The paintwork showed the characteristic style of the period.

'James? What's wrong?'

He reached out and touched the bauble gently, his finger tracing the painted flowers. 'Eleanor and I had one like this. Exactly like this. She bought it our first Christmas together and we hung it on our tree.' His voice had gone quiet, distant. 'I wonder what happened to it. After I... after Christmas Day. Mrs Barker probably packed everything away.'

Lucy's chest tightened. 'Would you like this one?'

'I can't. It probably costs…'

'I'm buying it.' She was already signalling to the stallholder. 'How much for this bauble?'

'That's Victorian, genuine article. Eighty pounds.'

'I'll take it.' Lucy handed over the money before James could protest. The stallholder wrapped it carefully in tissue paper and placed it in a small box.

'There.' Lucy gave James the box. 'Now you have it again.'

James held the box carefully, his throat working. 'You didn't have to do that.'

'I know. But I wanted to.' She touched his arm gently. 'Tell me about her, about Eleanor.'

For a moment, she thought he wouldn't answer. Then, quietly: 'She was a good person. Kind, patient, funny when you least expected it. She deserved better than dying at twenty-eight. Better than me as a husband, probably. I was always working.'

'You loved her.'

'I did. Very much. But I don't think I knew how to show it properly. I thought providing, working, being successful... I thought that was love. I thought if I could build a good practice, establish myself, give her a comfortable life, that would be enough.' He stared at the box in his hands. 'I didn't know how to just be present or how to stop working and sit with her, talk to her and enjoy the time we had and then she was gone and I realised I'd wasted it. All those hours I spent in my surgery when I could have been with her. All those evenings I came home late when she'd waited dinner for me. I was so focused on building a future that I forgot to live in the present.'

Lucy took his hand, threading her fingers through his. 'You can't change what happened with Eleanor. But you can change what you do now. How you choose to spend the time you have.'

'What time? I have four days, Lucy. I have four days until

my heart gives out, and I die alone in my surgery.' His fingers tightened around hers. 'Unless the passage has changed things or you've changed things. But we don't know, do we? We don't know if anything we've done makes a difference.'

Before Lucy could answer, a child's voice cut through the market noise. Crying, frightened, calling for his mum.

James's head snapped around immediately, his medical instincts overriding everything else. A little boy, perhaps five years old, stood near the Christmas tree sobbing. His face was red, his hands clutching a toy soldier.

'Lost,' James said, already moving. 'He's lost his mother.'

They reached the boy together. James knelt, bringing himself to the child's eye level. His voice shifted, becoming gentle, reassuring.

'Hello there. I'm James. What's your name?'

The boy hiccupped, tears streaming down his face. 'T-Tommy.'

'Tommy. That's a fine name. Are you lost, Tommy?'

A nod, more tears.

'That's all right. We'll find your mum. Can you tell me what she looks like? Is she wearing a special coat or hat?'

'She's got a red coat and a blue hat with a bobble.'

'Excellent. Very helpful. Now, Tommy, I need you to be very brave. Can you stay right here with my friend Lucy while I go and find your mum? Lucy is very nice, and she'll keep you safe.'

Lucy knelt beside them. 'I'll stay right here with you, Tommy. Your mum is probably just nearby, looking for you. We'll find her very quickly.'

James stood and caught Lucy's eye. 'I'll check the main paths. She can't have gone far.'

'Go. I've got him.'

James disappeared into the crowd. Lucy stayed with Tommy, distracting him with questions about the toy soldier he was holding, about what he wanted for Christmas, about whether he liked mince pies. Gradually, the crying subsided. Tommy's breathing steadied.

'Is that man a doctor?' Tommy asked. 'He talks like a doctor.'

'He is a doctor and a very good one, too.'

'My gran says doctors are clever. She says they know everything.'

'Well, not everything. But they know quite a lot.' Lucy smiled at him. 'Don't worry, he'll find your mum. He's very good at finding things.'

Three minutes later, James reappeared with a frantic woman in a red coat and blue bobbled hat. She spotted Tommy and burst into tears.

'Oh, thank God! Tommy, I told you to stay close!' She scooped him up, squeezing him tight. 'I turned around and you were gone. I've been terrified.'

'I'm sorry, Mummy. I wanted to see the big tree.'

'It's quite all right,' James said. 'He was very brave and told us exactly what you looked like so that I could find you.' He smiled at the boy. 'You did wonderfully, Tommy.'

The mother thanked them profusely, pressing a tenner into James's hand despite his protests. Then she carried Tommy away, still scolding and hugging him alternately.

James stared at the money in his hand. 'She gave me money for helping find her son.'

'People do that sometimes, express gratitude with money.' Lucy took his arm. 'You were wonderful with him. Natural, calm and reassuring. That's who you are, isn't it? When you're not drowning in patients and grief. That kind, gentle person who knows how to make frightened children feel safe.'

'I used to be better at it. Before Eleanor died and before I became so...' He trailed off.

'Lost? Exhausted? Self-destructive?'

'All of those.' He tucked the tenner into his pocket. 'But helping that boy felt good. It reminded me why I became a doctor in the first place. Not to punish myself or prove anything. Just to help people. Simple as that.'

'Simple as that,' Lucy echoed. 'Come on. Let's walk home. I think we've had enough Victorian inauthenticity for one day.'

Snow had started falling while they'd been at the market. Soft flakes drifted down, catching in James's dark hair, melting on his borrowed jacket. Otley looked beautiful under its white blanket, the modern town transformed into something almost timeless.

Walking beside James, their hands still linked from earlier, Lucy felt something shift in her chest. A warmth that had nothing to do with the walking or the mulled wine they'd drunk earlier. Something deeper, more complicated and considerably more dangerous.

She was falling for him. This brilliant, damaged, kind man from another century. This doctor who cared too much and loved too hard and was slowly killing himself trying to save everyone but himself.

When had it happened? When he'd knelt beside Tommy, his voice gentle and reassuring? When he'd held the bauble and talked about Eleanor with such raw honesty? When he'd corrected Victorian cooking techniques with barely suppressed glee? Or had it been gradual, building over days of shared work and conversations and learning to trust each other across an impossible divide?

It didn't matter when. What mattered was the reality: she was falling for him, and she had four days before she lost him forever.

Unless they changed things and the passage, the connection, the impossible love growing between them could somehow rewrite history. But how? What would that even look like? James staying in 2025, abandoning his patients and his life? Lucy going back to 1885, giving up everything she knew? Both options seemed impossible.

Yet she couldn't imagine letting him go or see herself standing in 2025 on Christmas Day knowing that in 1885, James was dying alone in his surgery. The thought made her chest ache.

'Lucy?' James squeezed her hand gently. 'You've gone quiet. What are you thinking?'

'Nothing important.' Too much to say standing in the snow on a street corner. 'I'm just glad you came today and that you let yourself have one morning off.'

'I'm glad too.' He smiled at her, snowflakes catching on his eyelashes. 'Thank you. For the market and the bauble and for reminding me that life can be more than just work and duty. I'd forgotten that. I think I forgot how to be James, just James, a person who could enjoy simple things like walking through a market on a winter's day.'

'You're remembering now, though. That's what matters.'

'Because of you. You're teaching me to live again. Ironic, isn't it? A woman from the future teaching a dying man how to live in the present.'

'You're not dying, not if I can help it.'

'Lucy...'

'We have four days to figure this out and to change what happens and we will, somehow.' She spoke with more confidence than she felt. 'You're eating better, sleeping more, sharing the workload and you're already stronger than you were a week ago. That has to count for something.'

'What if it's not enough? What if history is fixed, and all we're doing is waiting for the inevitable?' His voice was quiet, serious. 'What if on Christmas Day, my heart gives out anyway? Despite everything we've done?'

'Then at least we tried and you'll have had these days and these moments. That's better than dying without ever knowing what was possible.'

'Is it? I'm not sure. Sometimes I think it would have been easier not to know. Not to have met you, not to have seen what the future holds. Not to have...' He stopped walking and turned to face her. Snow fell around them, muffling the sounds of the town. 'Not to have fallen for you.'

Lucy's breath caught. 'James...'

'I know. It's foolish. We've known each other less than a week and we're from different centuries. Everything about this is impossible but I can't help it. You've reminded me what it feels like to care about someone and to want more than just the next patient, the next crisis. I want a future, even if I'm not sure I have one.' His hand came up to cup her face gently. 'You've given me hope, Lucy. Real hope, for the first time since Eleanor died. Whatever happens on Christmas Day, thank you for that.'

'You needed reminding. We both did.'

They walked the rest of the way in comfortable silence. At the house, James paused before going through the passage.

'I should check on patients this afternoon. But tonight, may I come back? To your time? I'd like to spend the evening here. With you, if that's all right.'

'Of course it's all right. I'll make dinner that is properly English this time, not just pasta.'

'You're going to cook for me twice in one week? I'm honoured.'

'Don't be. I'm a mediocre cook at best. But you need feeding, and I need something to do with my hands.' She hesitated, then said what she'd been thinking all day. 'James, we need to talk. About what happens after Christmas and the choice you'll need to make.'

His expression turned serious. 'I know. But not today. Let

me have today just being grateful and tomorrow we can face the hard conversations.'

'Tomorrow, then. Promise?'

'Promise.' He kissed her hand, a gesture so Victorian and so natural that it made her breath catch. 'Hard conversations postponed until tomorrow, let's have tonight.'

'Tonight,' Lucy agreed.

James stepped through the passage and was gone. Lucy stood in the library, staring at the bookcase, her hand still tingling where he'd kissed it.

She touched her hand where his lips had been and whispered to the empty room: 'Please let this work. Please.'

Outside, snow continued to fall, covering Otley in white. Covering the past and the future, 1885 and 2025, in the same soft blanket. Time moved forward, as it always does. But here, in this house, in this passage between moments, maybe time could be negotiated. Maybe history could be rewritten, and maybe love was enough to change everything.

Lucy hoped so. Because falling for James Ashworth was the most foolish, wonderful, terrifying thing she'd done in years.

THE NHS CRISIS

The phone rang at seven the next morning. Lucy was in the kitchen making coffee when Rachel's name flashed on the screen.

'Please tell me you're not still asleep,' Rachel said without preamble. 'Because I need a massive favour and I'm desperate enough to wake you if necessary.'

'I'm awake. What's wrong?'

'Everything. The whole hospital is falling apart. Winter flu has hit hard, half the staff are off sick, and A&E is overflowing into the corridors. We're calling everyone we can think of. Anyone with nursing experience who might help.' Rachel's voice was ragged with exhaustion. 'I know you were made redundant. I know this is probably the last thing you want to do. But Lucy, we're drowning. Can you come in? Just for one shift? Please?'

Lucy's stomach clenched. The hospital, her old hospital, the very place she'd been made redundant from.

'I don't know if I can.'

'You're still registered on the bank Lucy.'

'Yes, but...'

'Then you can. Lucy, people are waiting sixteen hours to be seen. We've got elderly patients on trolleys in hallways. I've been on shift for fourteen hours and I can't see straight anymore. I know it's a lot to ask and I know you're going through things. But we need you.'

Through the doorway, Lucy could see James emerging from the library, drawn by her voice. He was in Victorian clothes, having stayed overnight in 1885 and crossed through early. His hair was sleep-mussed, his waistcoat unbuttoned.

'Let me call you back,' Lucy said. 'Give me ten minutes.'

'Thank you. Even if you say no, thank you for considering it.' Rachel hung up.

James crossed to the kitchen, reading her expression. 'What's happened?'

'The hospital where I used to work are overwhelmed with a winter flu crisis. They need staff.' Lucy set down her phone with shaking hands. 'They want me to come in for a shift.'

'That's excellent. You should go.'

'I can't.'

'Why not?'

'Because I'll mess it up, I haven't worked in months and what if I'm not good enough anymore? What if I never was?' The words tumbled out before she could stop them. 'What if the redundancy was right? What if I really am useless?'

James caught her hands, stopping their trembling. His grip was warm and steady. 'Lucy. Look at me.'

She did, reluctantly.

'You've been telling me to stop punishing myself,' he said quietly. 'To accept that I'm worthy of living and to believe that I matter. Do you not see you're doing the same thing? Punishing yourself for something that wasn't your fault?'

'It's different.'

'It's exactly the same. You're a nurse and it's not just what you do, it's who you are. I've watched you work you're brilliant, competent, calm, intuitive. This redundancy, your divorce, they don't change that. They don't make you less capable or less worthy.' His thumbs rubbed circles on the backs of her hands. 'They need you; your friend needs you and I think you need this too. To remember what you're good at and to stop letting fear make your decisions.'

'When did you get so wise?'

'I have always been wise, and I have also been spending time with a very stubborn woman who refuses to let me give up. I'm simply returning the favour.' He smiled at her. 'Go now. Call your friend back and tell her yes.'

'What about your patients?'

'Mrs Barker can handle messages for one day. Anyone urgent can wait until evening. Besides, I'm coming with you.'

'James, you can't. You're not registered in this time; you can't practice modern medicine.'

'I won't practice. I'll observe, assist, learn. I've watched you work in my time. Let me watch you work in yours.' His expression turned serious. 'And selfishly, I want to see it. Modern medicine in practice. What I could be, if I lived. What the future of healing looks like.'

Lucy knew she should argue, and that it was complicated, potentially problematic. But the thought of walking into that hospital alone terrified her. Having James there, even just as support, made it bearable.

'All right. But you follow my lead. If I tell you to do something, you do it immediately. No questions, no debate.'

'Yes, Nurse Patterson.' He smiled. 'Now call your friend back before she has a nervous breakdown.'

Two hours later, they stood outside Leeds General Infirmary. The building was massive, modern, institutional.

Ambulances queued at the A&E entrance. Lucy could hear the chaos inside.

'That's a hospital?' James stared up at the building. 'It's enormous.'

'It's a Teaching hospital. One of the biggest in the region, it serves hundreds of thousands of people.' Lucy started toward the entrance, her heart hammering. 'Ready?'

'Probably not. But let's proceed anyway.'

The A&E department was bedlam. Every seat in the waiting room was filled. Patients sat on the floor, leaned against walls, and lay on trolleys in corridors. The reception desk was under siege from worried relatives. Children were screaming. The smell was unmistakable: disinfectant, illness and vomit.

Rachel spotted them immediately. She looked terrible, her scrubs rumpled, dark circles under her eyes, her hair escaping from its ponytail.

'Thank God.' She hugged Lucy hard. 'I could kiss you. Who's this?'

'James. He's, um, observing. Medical student, just shadowing me.' The lie came out smoother than expected. 'Is that all right?'

'Right now, I'd accept help from a trained monkey. Yes, it's fine. Come on, I'll get you both sorted.' Rachel led them through the chaos to the nurses' station. 'Lucy, you're on the medical assessment unit. We're using it as overflow from A&E. Basically, you're triaging, stabilising, and moving people through as fast as possible. James, you can assist. Fetch supplies, take obs, anything that doesn't require prescribing. Clear?'

'Crystal,' Lucy said.

Rachel thrust a pile of scrubs at them. 'Get changed, get to work. God knows we need you.'

In the changing room, Lucy pulled on the familiar blue

scrubs. They felt strange after so long away. Wrong and right simultaneously. James changed in the adjacent room, emerging looking thoroughly modern in scrubs and trainers that Lucy had found for him.

'How do I look?' he asked.

'Like a medical student who's about to get the education of his life.' Lucy took a deep breath. 'All right. Let's do this.'

The medical assessment unit was chaos incarnate. Twelve beds, all full. Three more patients on trolleys in the corridor. Two nurses covering the whole unit, both looking ready to collapse. When Lucy introduced herself, the relief on their faces was palpable.

'Take Bay Two,' one of them said. 'Four patients, all need assessing. Notes are on the board, such as they are. If you need anything, shout. Good luck.'

Bay Two held four elderly patients, all with respiratory symptoms. Lucy moved to the first bed, her training kicking in automatically. ABC. Airway, breathing, circulation. Check obs. Assess, prioritise, act.

The woman in the bed was perhaps seventy-five, her breathing laboured. Lucy checked her name on the notes: Mrs Patel. Admitted three hours ago with suspected pneumonia.

'Mrs Patel? I'm Lucy, one of the nurses. I'm going to check you over, all right?'

Mrs Patel nodded weakly. Lucy began her assessment, her hands steady despite her earlier panic. Pulse elevated. Blood pressure: slightly low. Temperature: 38.9. Oxygen saturation: 89 per cent on room air.

'James, can you get me an oxygen mask? Non-rebreather, fifteen litres. Ask someone to show you where to find it.'

He was back in less than a minute with the equipment. Lucy fitted the mask to Mrs Patel's face, adjusting the flow. Within moments, the woman's breathing eased slightly.

'Better?' Lucy asked.

Mrs Patel nodded again, some colour returning to her face.

Lucy moved to the next patient, James shadowing her. An elderly man, Mr Thompson, with heart failure. Fluid overload, lungs crackling, ankles swollen. She checked his drug chart and noted he was due for IV diuretics.

'James, find whoever's prescribing today. Tell them Bay Two, bed three needs furosemide urgently. Can you remember that?'

'Furosemide. Bay Two, bed three. Urgently.' He disappeared.

Third patient: Mrs Simmons, confused and dehydrated. Catheterised but not producing much urine. Possible UTI. Lucy checked her cannula, started fluids running faster, and made notes for the doctor.

Fourth patient: Mr Harrison, chest infection. Already on IV antibiotics but clearly struggling. Lucy adjusted his pillows, helping him sit more upright. His breathing eased marginally.

By the time she'd assessed all four, forty minutes had passed. Forty minutes that felt like both an eternity and an instant. Her hands were steady, and her mind was clear. All the fear, all the doubt, had evaporated the moment she'd started working.

This was what she was good at and who she was.

James reappeared with a doctor in tow, a harried-looking registrar who prescribed the necessary drugs, checked Lucy's notes, and nodded approvingly.

'Good work. Keep monitoring them and shout if anyone deteriorates.'

The next hours blurred together. Patient after patient, assessment after assessment. Lucy moved through them with increasing confidence, James always at her elbow. Fetching supplies, taking observations, holding hands, providing comfort. The staff assumed he was a student, and he played the role perfectly. Asking intelligent questions, watching protocols, learning by observation.

Around hour three, a new admission arrived. Mr Collins, mid-sixties, chest pain and shortness of breath. Possible cardiac event. Lucy took one look at his grey complexion and clammy skin and felt her training kick in harder.

'James, I need an ECG machine. Now.'

Whilst she attached the leads and ran the trace, she kept her voice calm and steady.

'You're doing fine, Mr Collins. Just try to relax for me. Can you tell me when the pain started?'

'About an hour ago. I thought it was indigestion at first.' His voice was breathless, frightened. 'But it keeps getting worse, like an elephant sitting on my chest.'

The ECG printed. Lucy looked at the trace and felt ice in her stomach. ST elevation in leads II, III, and aVF. Inferior MI. He was having a heart attack right now, this moment.

'I need the cardiac team!' she called out sharply. 'STEMI, Bay Two, bed one!'

Everything happened fast after that. The cardiac team descended, all efficiency and practiced coordination. Lucy handed over her notes, gave a concise summary, and stepped back to let the specialists take over. Mr Collins was whisked away for emergency angioplasty within minutes.

James stood beside her, watching the organised chaos with wide eyes. 'What's STEMI?'

'ST-elevation myocardial infarction. A heart attack. The ECG showed blocked coronary artery. They'll put in a stent, restore blood flow. In your time, he'd almost certainly die. In mine, he'll probably be home in a few days with medication and lifestyle advice.' She sagged against the wall briefly, adrenaline fading. 'That's the difference a century makes.'

'You saved his life. Recognised the symptoms immediately, acted without hesitation.' James looked at her with something like awe. 'In my time, I'd have bled him and given him laudanum and watched him die. Here, you've actually saved him.'

'Modern medicine saved him. I just knew what to look for.'

'Don't diminish what you did. That was extraordinary.'

At one point, Lucy found him sitting with Mrs Patel, holding her hand while she struggled through a particularly bad coughing fit.

'You're doing wonderfully,' he was saying in that gentle voice she recognised from when he'd comforted Tommy. 'Just breathe slowly. In through your nose, out through your mouth. That's it. Excellent.'

Mrs Patel's breathing eased. She looked at James with watery eyes. 'You're very kind. Are you a doctor?'

'Not quite yet. Still learning.' He smiled at her. 'But thank you.'

Across the bay, Lucy caught his eye. He was so good at this, natural, compassionate and intuitive. In Victorian clothes with Victorian tools, he was an excellent doctor. In modern scrubs in a modern hospital, he was just as good. Maybe better, because here he had the tools that actually worked along with medications that cured and equipment that saved lives.

What a waste, she thought. What an absolute waste for him to die in four days when he could have decades of this. Decades of helping people with tools that actually made a difference.

By hour six, Lucy's feet ached and her back hurt, but she felt more alive than she had in months. During a brief lull, the registrar pulled her aside.

'Your student is excellent. Natural bedside manner, good clinical instincts. Where's he studying?'

'Edinburgh.' The lie came easier each time.

'Well, tell him to apply here for foundation training. We could use people like him. He actually cares about patients as people, not just cases.' The registrar glanced back at James, who was helping Mr Thompson with his lunch, cutting up the food into manageable pieces. 'That's rarer than you'd think. Too many students these days are all about the exams and the prestige. This one genuinely wants to help, it really matters.'

Around hour nine, a young woman arrived, septic and deteriorating fast. Lucy took one look at the rapid respiratory rate, the mottled skin, the confusion, and moved immediately into action.

'Sepsis. I need the crash team, IV access, and fluids running. James, two wide-bore cannulas, now!'

She worked quickly, calling out orders, starting interventions. The crash team arrived and took over, but Lucy's early recognition and rapid treatment had bought crucial time. The young woman was whisked to ICU, critically ill but stabilised. Alive because Lucy had known what to look for and acted without hesitation.

'That's the second life you've saved today,' James said quietly afterward. 'How does it feel?'

'Like I'm doing what I'm meant to do.' Lucy realised it was true. For weeks, she'd felt useless, redundant in every sense of the word. But here, in the chaos, with patients who needed her skills and knowledge, she felt herself again. Competent, necessary and whole. 'Thank you for pushing me to come. I needed this more than I realised.'

By hour twelve, Rachel finally appeared and physically dragged Lucy away from the bay.

'Go home. You've done enough, more than enough.'

Rachel looked at her properly, taking in the flushed cheeks, the bright eyes, the energy despite the exhaustion. 'Weirdly, you look better than you have in months.'

'I feel better than I have in months.'

'You're a good nurse, Lucy. Never doubt that. Today proved it.' Rachel glanced at James, who was saying goodbye to Mrs Patel. 'Your student's good too. He's so gentle with patients, quick to learn, he'll make an excellent doctor.' Rachel hugged her. 'Thank you for coming. You saved us today. Literally. We wouldn't have coped without you.'

'Thank you for calling and reminding me why I do this.'

Outside, the winter evening had turned bitterly cold. Snow was falling again, covering the hospital car park in white. Lucy and James walked to her car in silence, both too exhausted for words.

Once inside, engine running for heat, they sat staring at the steering wheel.

'I'd forgotten,' Lucy said finally. 'That helping people feels so right. I'd made it into just... a job I lost. But it's more than that, it's who I am. Today reminded me.'

'You were extraordinary,' James said quietly. 'I watched you work. The calm under pressure, the clinical decisions, the way you prioritised and the compassion. You never forgot the person behind the patient and never treated them like just another case to process.'

'That's basic nursing.'

'It's excellent nursing. Many people have the knowledge but lack the humanity. You have both.' He turned to look at her. 'It's who you are, Lucy, just as it's who I am. It's not always about curing, sometimes it's just about being there. About holding someone's hand through the worst moments and reminding them they're not alone.'

'You were good too. Natural with patients and quick to learn. That registrar thought you were brilliant.' Lucy smiled tiredly. 'You'd make an excellent modern doctor, James. With proper training, modern knowledge, you'd be brilliant.'

He looked away, staring out at the falling snow. When he spoke, his voice was carefully neutral. 'Pity I'll be dead in four days.'

The words hit like ice water. Reality crashing back. For twelve hours, they'd been living in the present, focused on work and patients and the immediate needs of healing. They'd forgotten about Christmas, about fate, about the calendar counting down to an ending neither of them wanted to face.

'We don't know that' Lucy said, but even she could hear the doubt in her voice.

'Don't we? I've been eating better, sleeping more, sharing the workload and I feel better, genuinely and stronger. But Lucy, what if it's not enough? What if history is fixed and all we've done is give me a few more comfortable days before the inevitable?' He turned back to her, and his eyes were dark with something that looked like fear. 'Today was exhilarating. Working in that hospital, seeing modern medicine in action, watching you save lives with tools I can only dream of. It showed me what's possible. What I could do, what I could be, if I had a future. But I don't, do I? I have four days. Maybe less.'

'We could change it. We could…'

'How?' His voice rose slightly. 'How do we change it? I can't stay here permanently. I have no identity, no credentials, no legal existence in 2025. I'm a ghost and I can't abandon my patients in 1885. They need me. They're real people with real illnesses and no one else to help them.'

'Dr Fletcher takes over in January.'

'But only because I die. But what if I don't die? What if I choose to stay here? Who helps them?' James ran his hands through his hair, frustrated. 'And even if I could justify abandoning them, what kind of life would I have here? Pretending to be a medical student? Starting from scratch? Years of training before I can practice. I'd be forty-two before I could actually be a doctor again. That's assuming I can even get into medical school without proper documentation.'

'We'd figure it out. Solicitors, forged papers, something. People do it.'

'Do they? Do people from the nineteenth century successfully integrate into the twenty-first with no paper trail, no history, no proof they exist?' He laughed bitterly. 'I'd be undocumented. One background check away from arrest or God knows what.'

'Then I'll come back to 1885 with you. I'll stay. I can nurse there just as well as here.'

'And give up everything? Your time, your world, your friends? Lucy, you were brilliant today. You saved lives. I watched you work and it was like watching someone finally be who they're meant to be. I can't ask you to give that up.'

'You're not asking. I'm offering.'

'No.' His voice was firm. 'I won't let you sacrifice your life for mine. That's not love, that's self-destruction and we've both done enough of that already.'

Lucy felt tears prick her eyes. 'So, what, then? You go back to 1885 and die on Christmas Day? I stay here knowing I could have saved you but didn't. That's the plan?'

'I don't know!' James's voice cracked. 'I don't have a plan or answers. All I know is that today showed me what I want. I want to live, Lucy. I want decades of work like this. I want to save lives with antibiotics and oxygen and modern surgery and to hold your hand and take you to more markets and learn about your impossible future. I want all of it, but wanting doesn't make it possible.'

'Maybe it does.'

'Or maybe I'm just postponing the inevitable. That my heart will give out on Christmas Day regardless of what I eat or how much I sleep or how desperately I want to survive.' He leaned back against the headrest, exhausted. 'I'm sorry, I shouldn't have said all that. Today was wonderful and you were wonderful. I just... I saw what could be and realising I can't have it is harder than never knowing it existed.'

Lucy reached over and took his hand. 'We have four days to figure something out. To find a solution.'

'And if we can't?'

'Then at least we tried. At least you'll have had these days. These moments.' She squeezed his hand. 'I'm not giving up on you, James. Not after watching you with those patients and seeing how good you are at this. The world needs you; modern medicine needs you. I need you.'

He turned to look at her, and in his eyes, she saw hope and despair tangled together. 'I need you too. That's the problem. I've spent a year telling myself I didn't need anyone, that losing Eleanor meant I should never let myself care again and then you appeared in my library wearing peculiar clothes from an impossible time, and everything changed. You made me care and now I have to face the possibility that I might lose you just as I've found you.'

'You're not losing me. Not yet.' Lucy started the car. 'Come on. Let's go home. We're both exhausted and emotional. Tomorrow we'll think clearly.'

'Tomorrow,' James echoed. But he didn't sound convinced.

They drove back to Otley in silence; the snow falling steadily around them. Through the windscreen, the road ahead looked uncertain, obscured by weather and darkness. Behind them, the hospital glowed with electric light, full of people being saved by modern medicine.

Lucy gripped the steering wheel tighter and drove

through the snow, refusing to cry. Crying wouldn't help or change anything.

'We'll figure it out,' she said aloud. 'Somehow we have to.'

James didn't answer. But his hand found hers on the gearstick and held on tight.

THE HARD TRUTH

*D*ecember 22nd. Three days until James Ashworth was supposed to die in his surgery, alone, his heart giving out after months of self-destruction.

Lucy woke early, the weight of the calendar pressing down on her. Through the bedroom window, Otley was grey under low clouds. Rain threatened, that cold December rain that soaked through everything.

Downstairs, she found James already in the library, sitting in the leather chair by the cold fireplace. Still in Victorian clothes from last night, when he'd gone back to check on patients. He looked tired, thoughtful, his hands wrapped around a cup of tea that had gone cold.

'Couldn't sleep?' Lucy asked from the doorway.

He looked up, managing a small smile. 'Too much thinking. You?'

'Same.' She came in and sat on the sofa facing him. 'We need to talk, don't we? About what happens in three days.'

'Yes.' James set down his cup carefully. 'But we're running out of chances to figure this out.'

'What have you been thinking?'

'Everything. Every possibility, every option, every outcome.' He leaned forward, elbows on his knees. 'If I go back, if I try to change things by taking better care of myself, eating properly, sleeping, reducing my workload... what then? Let's say it works. Let's say I live past Christmas Day. I survive a few more years, maybe decades.'

'That's good, isn't it? That's what we want.'

'But Lucy, you're here. In 2025. We'd never see each other again except through the passage. Once a month? Once a week? Stolen moments across 140 years?' His voice was tight with frustration. 'That's not a life. Knowing you exist but I can't be with you. After having tasted what we could have together and then spending the rest of my life alone, remembering.'

'The passage might stay open. We could visit...'

'For how long? An hour? A day? And then what? I go back to gaslit rooms and patients I can't save, whilst you stay here with electric light and antibiotics and the future I'll never see?' He stood abruptly, pacing. 'I've thought about this, imagined what it would be like. Coming here to see you, spending a few precious hours together, then having to leave. Again, and again and never able to build a real life together.'

Lucy felt her throat tighten. 'What's the alternative?'

James stopped pacing and turned to face her. 'I could stay here with you.'

The words hung in the air between them. Outside, the first drops of rain began to fall.

'Stay,' Lucy repeated. 'In 2025. Permanently.'

'Yes.' He crossed back to sit beside her on the sofa, close enough that their knees touched. 'I've been thinking about this since the hospital. Lucy, I could live here. I could learn modern medicine, train again, be a doctor in a time when I can actually save people instead of just watching them die.'

'You'd have to start completely over. No credentials, no identity, nothing.'

'I know and seven years of training before I could practice.' He took her hands, his grip warm and urgent. 'But I'd have those seven years and decades after that. I could have a life with you, if you want that. Instead of dying alone on Christmas Day, I could stay here and build something real.'

Lucy wanted to say yes. Wanted it so desperately it physically hurt. But she forced herself to be rational, to think clearly.

'What about your patients? The people who need you in 1885?'

'They need someone but not me specifically. I was going to die anyway, remember? Dr Fletcher arrives in January to take over. Someone will fill the gap.' His hands tightened on hers. 'I know that sounds callous and I know my patients are real people with real needs. But Lucy, I can't save everyone. If I stay in 1885, I die and they get Fletcher anyway. At least this way, I live and get to have a future instead of becoming a footnote in local history.'

'You'd be giving up everything you know. Your entire world along with your identity as Dr Ashworth, respected physician and you'd become nobody. An illegal immigrant with no papers, no past, no proof you exist.'

'Better to be nobody in 2025 than dead in 1885.' He almost smiled, but it didn't reach his eyes. 'Besides, I'd be somebody to you. Isn't that enough?'

'James, we've known each other a week and you're talking about giving up your entire life for me?'

'Not just for you but also for me.' He released one of her hands to gesture around the room. 'Look at what I've seen this past week. Electric light, central heating, food that doesn't spoil immediately. Medicine that actually works so that people go on living into their eighties and nineties instead of dying at forty. Lucy, in your time, the things that kill my patients are preventable. I could learn to wield that power, those tools. I could spend decades saving lives that would be lost in my own time.'

'You could. But it would take years of study and pretending to be someone you're not. Constantly living in constant fear of discovery.'

'We'd figure it out. People integrate into new identities all the time.'

'Do they? Do Victorian doctors successfully convince immigration officials they're legitimate 21st-century citizens?' Lucy pulled her hands away gently. 'James, I want this. God, I want this so much. But I need you to really think about what you'd be giving up. Not just patients and practice but your whole world. Mrs Barker, your house, your friends, everything familiar. You'd be completely alone except for me.'

'I'm already alone and I have been since Eleanor died.' His voice went quiet. 'Do you know what the last year has been like? Waking up every morning to emptiness. Working myself into exhaustion because at least then I'm too tired to feel anything. Coming home to a house that used to have warmth and laughter but now just echoes. I've been alone in 1885, Lucy. At least here, with you, I'd have a reason to be alive.'

'What if it doesn't work? What if you come to resent me for it? For taking you away from everything you knew?'

'What if it does work? What if this is exactly what we're both meant to do?' James turned to face her fully. 'You've spent months punishing yourself for losing your job. Convincing yourself that you're a failure and that you don't matter. But you do matter, I saw you at that hospital. You saved lives and made a difference, and I think you need someone who sees you for who you really are, not who you think you should be.'

'And you need someone to remind you that you're allowed to live. That surviving Eleanor's death doesn't mean you have to die too.'

'Exactly. So maybe we're perfect for each other. Two broken people who can help each other heal.' He smiled sadly and genuinely. 'Or maybe I'm being completely foolish and I'm simply making a massive decision based on a week's acquaintance and feelings that are too intense to be rational.'

'Are they rational? These feelings?' Lucy asked quietly.

'No. Nothing about this is rational. Time travel isn't rational. Falling in love with someone from 140 years in the future isn't rational. Wanting to abandon my entire life for a chance at happiness isn't rational.' He met her eyes steadily. 'But it's what I want, I want to live, Lucy and I want to stop existing in grief and actually live. With you, if you'll have me.'

'Of course I want that. But James, what if you stay and something goes wrong? What if history can't be changed and your heart gives out anyway? What if the passage closes and you're trapped here with no way back?'

'Then at least I'll have tried and I'll have chosen life over death. Isn't that better than just accepting fate?'

Lucy stood and walked to the window. Rain streaked the glass, distorting the view of the street outside. Somewhere in 1885, it was possibly raining too. The same weather in the same town, separated by 140 years and an impossible choice.

'I'm scared,' she admitted. 'Terrified, actually. What if I'm not enough? What if you stay and realise you've made a terrible mistake and end up hating me for encouraging this?'

'I could never hate you.' James came to stand beside her. 'But I understand the fear. I'm scared too, scared of dying and of living. Scared of making the wrong choice and regretting it forever. But Lucy, I'm more scared of not choosing and letting fear decide for me.'

'When did you decide this? That you wanted to stay?'

'At the hospital when I was watching you work, seeing what modern medicine could do. When holding that woman's hand whilst you saved her from a heart attack that would have killed her in my time.' His reflection in the window looked haunted. 'I realised I didn't want to go back.'

'You'd be giving up so much.'

'I'd be gaining more.' He turned to look at her directly. 'Unless you don't want that. If you'd rather I go back, if this is too much, too fast, I'll understand. I'll return to 1885 and try to take better care of myself. We can visit through the passage when possible. But I need to know what you want, Lucy. Not what you think I should do, or what's practical, or what makes sense. What do you want?'

What did she want? Lucy stared at their reflections in the rain-streaked glass. Two people who shouldn't exist together, who'd found each other across an impossible divide. A Victorian doctor and a 21st-century nurse, both running from grief, both trying to find a reason to keep going.

'I want you to stay,' she said quietly. 'I want it so much it terrifies me. But James, I need you to be certain. Absolutely certain. Because if you stay and regret it, I'll never forgive myself. I need you to choose this for you, not for me.'

'I'm certain.' His voice was steady, sure. 'I've spent a year wanting to die. Pushing myself toward collapse because it seemed easier than living without Eleanor and then you appeared in my library, impossible and brave and completely alive. You reminded me what it feels like to want something.'

'Eleanor,' Lucy said. 'We need to talk about her.'

'What about her?'

'You loved her and you're still grieving her. How do I

know this isn't just... transference? Replacing one person with another because you can't bear the emptiness?'

James was quiet for a long moment. Rain continued its steady drumming against the window. Somewhere in the house, a floorboard creaked. When he spoke, his voice was thoughtful, measured.

'Eleanor was my wife, and I loved her deeply, completely. I failed her by not being present enough, by working too much and taking her for granted. When she died, I thought I should die too. I felt that I didn't deserve to be happy again and that seeking joy after losing her would somehow be a betrayal of what we had.' He turned Lucy to face him gently. 'But you're not Eleanor. She was gentle and patient where you're direct and fierce, she accepted my workaholic tendencies where you challenge them head-on. She wanted a quiet domestic life where you want purpose and meaning and constant challenge.'

'I'm not sure that's a compliment.'

'It is. You're exactly what I need right now. Someone who won't let me hide in work, who'll push me to take care of myself.' He smiled. 'Eleanor would have liked you, she wanted me to slow down, but I never listened properly, and I think she'd want me to be happy and to find someone who makes me want to live, not just exist.'

'You think she'd approve of you abandoning 1885? Leaving your patients, your life, everything you built together?'

'I think she'd tell me to stop being a martyr and accept help when it's offered. She was eminently practical and used to say I had a gift for making everything harder than it needed to be. That I'd work myself into an early grave if I wasn't careful.' His laugh was hollow. 'Turns out she was right about that.'

'This isn't about replacing her, though? You're sure of that?'

'I'm sure. Grief doesn't work that way. You don't replace people you've lost but you do carry them with you and eventually learn to live alongside the loss.' His expression turned serious again. 'This isn't about replacing Eleanor. It's about choosing a future; she wouldn't want me to die young just because she did. That's not love.'

Lucy felt tears prick her eyes. 'We have three days to decide if we're really doing this.'

'I've decided. I'm staying. The question is whether you want me to.'

'Of course I do. But James, it's not that simple. Where will you live? How will you support yourself? What about documentation, education, all the practical things?'

'We'll figure it out. One step at a time.' He pulled her close, wrapping his arms around her. 'I know it's mad, impulsive, foolish and definitely complicated. But I don't care. I'm choosing life with you if you'll let me.'

Lucy buried her face in his shoulder, breathing in the faint scent of carbolic soap and wool. Victorian smells that shouldn't exist in 2025 but did, because time had bent itself around them.

'All right,' she whispered. 'All right, stay, we'll figure out the rest.'

She felt him sag slightly, relief making his shoulders drop. 'Thank you. I won't let you regret this. I promise.'

'Don't make promises you can't keep. Just promise you won't die on Christmas Day. That's all I need.'

'I promise. No dying on Christmas. Or any other day soon, if I can help it.' He pulled back to look at her, his eyes bright. 'So, what now? What do we do with these three days?'

'We make sure you're strong enough to survive and we plan. But first, you need to go back to 1885 and check on your patients, make sure everything's stable. Say goodbye properly, even if they won't know that's what you're doing.'

'Goodbye.' James tested the word. 'I'll be saying goodbye to everything, my house, my practice, my life and to Mrs Barker who has been with me since I was a boy. How do I say goodbye to her?'

'Carefully. Honestly, if you can. She cares about you and deserves to know you're all right, even if she can't understand how.'

'She'll think I'm mad.'

'She already thinks you're mad. This will just confirm it.' Lucy managed a watery smile. 'Go. Take today. Check on everyone, make your peace with 1885. The day after tomorrow is Christmas Eve; we'll make our final preparations. And Christmas Day...'

'Christmas Day, I stay here. With you and we start building a life together.'

'A very complicated, probably illegal, definitely unconventional life.'

'The best kind.' James kissed her forehead gently. 'Thank you for giving me hope.'

'Thank you for helping me to be brave enough to choose life.'

'We're both choosing life. That's rather poetic, isn't it?'

'It's something.' Lucy pulled away reluctantly. 'Go on. Your patients need you. Mrs Barker probably has questions about where you've been, and I need to think about practical things like where you're going to live and how we explain a Victorian doctor appearing in 2025.'

'Those are concerning practical details, yes.'

'We'll manage somehow because we have to.' She walked him to the passage door. 'Tonight? Will you come back tonight?'

'Wild horses couldn't keep me away. Or wild motor vehicles or whatever the modern equivalent is.' He paused at the door. 'Lucy, I mean it. I'm staying, I've made my choice.'

'I know. I believe you.' And she did. Whatever happened next, whatever complications arose, James Ashworth was choosing life and choosing her.

He stepped into the passage. Lucy watched him disappear into the darkness, then closed the door and the bookcase behind him.

RESEARCH

Lucy couldn't sleep. At three in the morning, she'd given up trying and gone downstairs with her laptop. If James was really staying, if they were really doing this, she needed to know what would happen in 1885. What consequences his choice would create.

Now, at dawn, she sat surrounded by printouts and notes. Historical records, newspaper archives, census data. Everything she could find about Otley in 1885 and 1886 and about Dr James Ashworth and what occurred after his death.

Through the passage, it was probably morning in 1885 too. James would be checking on patients, making his rounds. Saying goodbye to a world he'd decided to leave behind.

Lucy returned to her research. The Otley Historical Society's website had been invaluable. Someone had digitised old newspapers, census records, death certificates. The detail was extraordinary and slightly unsettling.

'Dr James Ashworth (1850-1885) died unexpectedly on Christmas Day 1885,' one article read. 'The cause of death was determined to be heart failure, likely exacerbated by exhaustion and poor nutrition. Dr Ashworth had been working tirelessly throughout the recent fever outbreak, often at the expense of his own health. The community mourns the loss of a dedicated physician who put his patients' needs above his own well-being.'

The newspaper article was dated December 28th, 1885. Three days after his supposed death. Lucy read it twice, looking for details. No mention of how he was found, who discovered the body. Just the bare facts: died Christmas Day, heart failure, much mourned by the community.

Lucy clicked through more records and found another article from January 15th, 1886.

'The late Dr Ashworth's practice has been taken over by Dr William Fletcher, recently arrived from Edinburgh. Dr Fletcher comes highly recommended and brings modern ideas about hygiene and sanitation. The community welcomes this skilled practitioner during our time of need.'

More digging revealed Fletcher's impressive record. Within three months of arriving, he'd reorganised the local medical services. Improved sanitation in the poorest areas and set up a system for tracking infectious diseases. When a scarlet fever outbreak hit in March 1886, Fletcher's interventions saved dozens of lives.

'Dr Fletcher's modern approach to disease prevention has proven invaluable,' gushed an article from April 1886. 'Where Dr Ashworth worked heroically but ultimately could not stem the tide of illness, Dr Fletcher has implemented systematic improvements that address root causes. The community's health has improved markedly under his care.'

Lucy sat back, processing. If James died as history recorded, Fletcher arrived and was arguably better for the community. More organised, more preventative in his approach. Less likely to work himself to death because he understood the value of sustainable practice.

The patients would be fine. Better than fine, potentially.

What about Mrs Barker?

Census records from 1891 showed Martha Barker, aged 67, living in York with her daughter's family. Occupation: none. Status: mother-in-law. The 1901 census showed her still there, aged 77, described as 'elderly relative'. She died in 1910, age 85, having lived comfortably with her daughter for 24 years.

Lucy printed everything and made neat piles. Evidence of what happened in 1885. Proof that the world survived without James Ashworth.

Footsteps on the stairs, and James appeared in the kitchen doorway.

'You're up,' he said, taking in her dishevelled appearance, the laptop, the printouts scattered across the table. 'Did you sleep at all?'

'Not really.' Lucy gestured at the papers. 'I've been researching. What happens in 1885 if you don't go back. If you stay here.'

James crossed to the table slowly, looking at the printouts. 'What did you find?'

'Everything. The newspaper article about your death. Fletcher's arrival. Mrs Barker's fate. All of it.' She handed him the first article. 'Read.'

He did, silently. His face remained carefully neutral as he worked through the papers, reading about his own death and its aftermath. When he finished, he set them down carefully and sat across from her.

'So,' he said quietly. 'The world continues without me. Dr Fletcher arrives, implements better systems, saves more lives than I could have. Mrs Barker lives comfortably with her daughter for decades. Everyone is fine.'

'Yes.'

'I'm not indispensable after all. Just another person who

dies and gets replaced. Life goes on.' His voice was flat, but Lucy could hear something underneath. Pain, perhaps. Or relief.

'Everyone's replaceable in the grand scheme,' Lucy said gently. 'No one is so special that the world stops turning without them. That's not a criticism. It's just truth. Fletcher arrives because there's a gap. Whether that gap is created by death or departure doesn't matter to the outcome.'

'So, my choice doesn't create disaster. I won't be abandoning my patients to suffer and die.'

'No. Fletcher will be there within a month. Possibly sooner if he hears there's a practice available. Your patients will be cared for, probably better than you could manage whilst working yourself to death.'

James picked up the article about Fletcher's scarlet fever interventions and read it again. 'He saves dozens during the outbreak. I would have lost most of them because I didn't know about his preventative methods, his hygiene protocols. He's simply better at this than I am.'

'He just has more recent knowledge, had more time to research than you have. That doesn't diminish what you've done.'

'Doesn't it? If I stay with you and if Fletcher arrives earlier because I've left rather than died, he saves more lives. The community benefits from having a doctor who isn't half-dead from grief and exhaustion.' James looked up at her. 'Perhaps my staying here is actually the more moral choice. Perhaps I'm helping more people by stepping aside for someone more competent.'

'That's one way to look at it.'

'What's the other way?'

'That you're trying to rationalise a decision you've already made. Looking for permission to choose life instead of martyrdom.' Lucy reached across the table to take his hand. 'James, you don't need moral justification for wanting to live and you don't have to prove that staying in 2025 is somehow better for humanity than dying in 1885. You're allowed to choose survival and be selfish, for once.'

James was quiet for a long moment, staring at their joined hands. Outside, morning traffic increased. People were going about their ordinary December days, unaware that two time-crossed people were having an extraordinary conversation in an ordinary kitchen.

'Do you want to stay because you want to live? Because you want to be here, with me, building something impossible?'

'Yes.' There was no hesitation. 'Yes, I want to stay. I want to live for decades instead of days. I want to learn modern medicine and save lives with tools that work. But, more than anything, I want to wake up beside you and know I have a future.'

'Then that's enough. The rest, Fletcher and Mrs Barker and the community, they're just details. The important thing is that you're choosing life.'

'I'm choosing you.'

'You're choosing yourself. I'm just a very good incentive.' Lucy smiled tiredly. 'And I'm choosing you too, for what it's worth. Choosing to believe that love doesn't follow timelines or logic.'

James stood and came around the table, pulling her to her feet and into his arms. Lucy leaned against him. 'Are you scared?' she asked against his shoulder.

'Terrified. But also excited and hopeful.' He pulled back to look at her. 'What about you? Are you having second thoughts about harbouring a Victorian fugitive?'

'Occasional third and fourth thoughts, but the core decision remains the same. I want you here and I want us.' She touched his face gently. 'Though we do need to have some serious conversations about practicalities. Like where you'll live, how we explain you, what we tell people.'

'Can I stay here? In this house? It's technically mine, after all. I owned it in 1885. Surely that counts for something.'

'I'm not sure Victorian property ownership transfers across time. But it's a nice thought.' Lucy considered. 'Actually, you could stay here. The house is mine through an inheritance and if anyone asks, you're a friend staying whilst looking for accommodation. We can claim you're between flats.'

'Between flats and between centuries. Close enough.' James smiled. 'What about documentation? How do I prove I exist in 2025?'

'We'll need a solicitor. Someone who handles complex cases. There must be precedents for people without proper papers. Refugees, stateless individuals, complicated adoptions. We'll find someone who asks minimal questions and charges maximum fees.'

'That sounds expensive.'

'We'll manage.' Lucy pulled away to start gathering the research papers. 'But first, you need to talk to Mrs Barker, if you can. Give her some kind of closure, even if she doesn't understand.'

'Mrs Barker knows something's happening, she keeps giving me peculiar looks. She asked me yesterday if I was planning something foolish.'

'What did you tell her?'

'That I was planning something wonderful, but she didn't seem convinced.'

'To be fair, abandoning your century probably qualifies as both foolish and wonderful.'

'True.' James set down the papers and turned to her. 'Lucy, I need to ask something. Do you want me to stay, really?'

She met his eyes steadily. 'I want you to stay because I'm falling in love with you, and I know it's too soon and too fast and too impossible, but it's happening anyway. So yes. Stay. Please.'

James kissed her then, soft and sweet and desperate. When they pulled apart, they were both slightly breathless.

'I'm falling in love with you too,' he said quietly. 'Have been since you appeared in my library wearing those clothes and refusing to let me work myself to death and, if not then, it was the moment you called me out for being insufferable about Victorian Christmas markets.'

'That was a good moment. You were being extraordinarily pedantic.'

'I was being accurate. There's a difference.'

'There really isn't.' Lucy smiled against his mouth. 'Go back to 1885 for today. Tonight, come back here for good. And Christmas Day...'

'Christmas Day, I wake up in 2025. Alive and with you.' He kissed her forehead. 'That's a good Christmas present.'

'The best. Much better than dying alone in your surgery.'

'The bar is admittedly quite low.'

'True. But we'll clear it anyway.' She walked him to the library and the passage. 'Tonight, and don't make me come through and drag you back.'

'You wouldn't dare.'

'Try me. I've dragged non-compliant patients to treatment before. I'm not above doing it again.'

'Terrifying woman. No wonder I love you.' James stepped into the passage, then turned back. 'Thank you for doing the research, it makes it all easier.'

'That's why I did it. I needed you to know you weren't abandoning people to suffer.'

Lucy closed the bookcase and stood in the quiet library. Printouts about James's death and Fletcher's arrival lay on the table, evidence of a future that wouldn't happen. History rewriting itself because two people had fallen in love across an impossible divide.

Lucy gathered the papers and took them to the kitchen. Made herself breakfast and then took a shower, though she was too tired to care. She tried to nap, though her mind was racing with logistics and plans and the terrifying joy of knowing James was staying.

Tonight, he'd return, and on Christmas Day they'd wake up together and start building an impossible life.

CHRISTMAS EVE

James stood in his library in 1885, looking around at the room that had been his sanctuary for a decade. Wood-panelled walls, leather-bound medical texts, the desk where he'd written thousands of patient notes. Gaslight flickered on the mantelpiece, casting warm shadows. The fire in the grate crackled softly.

This had been home, and tomorrow, it wouldn't be.

He started with the patients. Timothy Dawson first, still recovering from the fever but vastly improved. The boy was sitting up in bed when James arrived, eating porridge whilst his mother fussed.

'Dr Ashworth!' Mrs Dawson's face lit up. 'Look at him! He's eating properly. Colour back in his cheeks. You've worked a miracle.'

'No miracle. Just good nursing care and time.' James examined Timothy, noting the clear eyes, the steady pulse, the lungs that sounded properly clear. 'He's doing wonderfully. Keep feeding him nourishing food, make sure he rests. He'll be running about with his brothers within a week.'

'Thank you, doctor. We thought we'd lost him. Truly we did.'

James thought of Lucy, her calm competence as they'd worked together on this case. Modern nursing knowledge combined with his Victorian practice. Together, they'd saved this child.

'He's a fighter,' James said. 'Keep him warm, keep him fed. He'll be fine.'

Next was Mrs Smith. James found her sitting in a rocking chair, a tiny bundle in her arms. She looked exhausted but radiant.

'Dr Ashworth, come see. Come see my girl.' She shifted the blanket to reveal a small, wrinkled face. 'Born yesterday morning, she's perfect. Absolutely perfect.'

James examined the baby with gentle hands. Good colour, strong cry, nursing well. Mother's recovery proceeding normally. Both healthy, both safe.

'She's beautiful,' he said honestly. 'What's her name?'

'Eleanor. After your late wife, if you don't mind. You've been so kind to us, so patient. I wanted to honour her memory.'

James felt his eyes fill. 'I don't mind at all. Eleanor would be honoured, she loved babies.'

'Will you be her godfather? My husband and I, we'd be proud if you'd stand for her at the christening.'

He almost said yes. Almost agreed without thinking and then reality hit.

'I'm afraid I can't. I'm... I'll be away. I'm going travelling for some time.' The lie tasted bitter. 'But I'm honoured you'd ask. Truly.'

Mrs Smith looked disappointed but nodded. 'Well, when you return then, you'll always be welcome in our home, doctor.'

James completed his rounds methodically. Mr Thompson, heart failure controlled. Mrs Simmons, confusion resolved with proper hydration. Mr Harrison, chest infection improving. All stable. All on the mend.

Back at his house, James went to his study and sat at the desk. The desk where he'd written patient notes, medical articles, letters to colleagues. Eleanor had sometimes sat reading whilst he worked, keeping him company in comfortable silence.

He pulled out fresh paper and began writing. Detailed notes on every current patient. Symptoms, treatments, responses, what to watch for. Instructions for ongoing care. Names and addresses. Family situations. Who could afford to pay and who couldn't but needed treatment anyway.

Everything Dr Fletcher would need to take over smoothly.

Page after page of careful notes. Everything he knew, everything he'd learned, every insight about his patients and their needs. A decade of practice distilled into precise instructions.

When he finished, it was late afternoon. His hand ached from writing, and the stack of papers on the desk was substantial.

James tied them with string and wrote on the top page: 'For Dr Fletcher, or whoever assumes care of these patients. All information current as of 24th December 1885. James Ashworth, MRCS.'

The sound of footsteps approaching came from the hallway. Mrs Barker appeared in the doorway, her face drawn with worry.

'Dr Ashworth, you've been in here for hours, you haven't eaten anything.' She came closer, seeing the papers on the desk. 'What are you doing? Those look like patient notes.'

'I am organising things and making sure everything's in order.'

'Why?' Her voice sharpened. 'Dr Ashworth, what's happening? You've been acting strangely for days. Disappearing for hours, coming back, talking about the future in ways that don't make sense and now you're organising your notes like... like you're preparing to leave.'

James set down his pen and looked at her. Mrs Barker had been with his family since he was born. She'd helped raise him after his mother died and cared for him through Eleanor's death. She deserved honesty, even if she wouldn't understand.

'I am leaving,' he said quietly. 'I am going somewhere that I can't explain. But it is somewhere I'll be happy.'

Mrs Barker's eyes filled with tears. 'You're leaving. I knew it. I don't know how I knew, but I did. That woman, the strange one in trousers. This is because of her, isn't it?'

'Her name is Lucy and yes, she's given me a reason to live again. A reason to hope and to believe I deserve a future.' James stood and crossed to the housekeeper. 'Mrs Barker, I've been dying slowly since Eleanor passed. You've watched me work myself toward collapse and you have tried so hard to save me, and I wouldn't let you. But Lucy... she's shown me what's possible.'

'Where are you going? Can you not tell me?'

'I can't explain and you wouldn't believe me if I tried. But I promise you, I'll be safe. I'll be cared for, and I'll be living properly for the first time in a year.'

'And what about us? What about your patients and this house?'

'A new doctor will arrive. Dr Fletcher. He's young, skilled, better than I am in many ways. I've left notes with everything he needs.' James took her hands gently. 'And there's money in an account for you. Enough for years of comfort. Promise me you'll use it. Go to your daughter in York and live comfortably. You've worked hard your whole life, and you deserve rest.'

'I don't want money. I want you to stop being foolish and stay where you belong.'

'I belong with Lucy. In a place where I can heal, where I can build instead of destroying myself.' His voice cracked slightly. 'Please understand. I'm not abandoning you, but I am saving myself. There's a difference.'

Mrs Barker pulled her hands away and wiped her eyes roughly. 'You're determined, then. Nothing I say will change your mind.'

'Nothing.'

'Then go.' Her voice was fierce. 'Go and be happy. Lord knows you deserve it after this year. If this Lucy can make you want to live, then go to her. I'll manage here and I'll make sure your patients are cared for until the new doctor arrives.'

'Thank you.' James pulled her into a hug, brief and tight. 'Thank you for everything, for raising me, caring for me and never giving up on me even when I'd given up on myself.'

'Foolish boy,' she said against his shoulder. 'Always were too hard on yourself. Too determined to save everyone except yourself. I'm glad someone finally got through to you.'

They stood there for a moment, two people who'd known each other for decades, saying goodbye without quite saying the word.

'I'll leave a letter,' James said, pulling back. 'In the desk. For whoever needs to handle my affairs. It'll explains everything. Well, as much as can be explained.' He paused. 'It'll tell people I've gone travelling, that I needed a change because I couldn't bear staying in Otley after Eleanor. They'll believe that.'

'Will you write? Let me know you're safe?'

'I can't promise that. Where I'm going, letters are...

complicated.' He smiled sadly. 'But I'll be thinking of you always. You've been more of a mother to me than my own, I hope you know that.'

'I know.' She straightened, pulling herself together with visible effort. 'Go on, then. Before I change my mind and lock you in your room like I did when you were twelve and tried to run away to sea.'

'You wouldn't.'

'Try me.' But she was smiling through tears. 'God go with you, Dr Ashworth. Be happy, safe and be everything you deserve to be.'

'I'll try.' James kissed her cheek. 'Goodbye, Mrs Barker. Thank you for everything.'

He left before he could lose his nerve. He walked through the house one last time, looking at everything with new eyes. The kitchen, where Mrs Barker had made him countless meals he hadn't eaten. The sitting room where Eleanor had done her needlework. The bedroom they'd shared, now cold and unused.

Goodbye. All of it. Goodbye.

In the library, the passage waited. James could see Lucy on the other side, standing in her dusty 2025 library, watching for him.

One last thing. James pulled paper from the desk and wrote quickly.

'To whom it may concern: I, Dr James Ashworth, being of sound mind and body, have decided to leave Otley. Recent events have made it impossible for me to continue practising here. I have made notes for a replacement physician to assume care of my patients. My housekeeper, Mrs Martha Barker, should receive all funds remaining in my accounts. This house and its contents I leave to any blood relatives that are found. May whoever lives here find peace. James Ashworth, 24th December 1885.'

Not entirely honest, but close enough. He left the letter on the desk where it would be found.

Then James Ashworth walked through the passage for the last time. From gaslight to electric light. From 1885 to 2025. From death to life.

Lucy met him on the other side, taking his hands. 'How did it go?'

'As well as could be expected. Everyone's stable. Mrs Barker knows I'm leaving. She gave me her blessing, more or less.' He looked back at the passage, still open. 'That's it, I've said goodbye. Left notes, letters, everything they need. There's nothing keeping me in 1885 anymore.'

'Are you alright?'

'I don't know.' James leaned against her, exhausted. 'It feels enormous, but also right. Like I'm finally making a choice for myself instead of just letting fate decide.'

'You are. You're choosing life.' Lucy held him close. 'Come on. We have decorating to do.'

'Decorating?'

'It's Christmas Eve. We need to make this house properly festive so let's do it properly.'

The tree was in the sitting room, a small real pine that Lucy had bought from a market stall. It stood bare and slightly crooked in the corner, reproachful in its nakedness.

'It needs work,' James observed.

'Everything needs work. That's the point.' Lucy produced boxes of decorations from a cupboard. Baubles, tinsel, fairy lights. 'The Victorian bauble goes on first. It will always have the place of honour.'

James took the bauble they'd bought at the market. The glass caught the electric light, the painted flowers glowing. Eleanor's bauble. Or close enough.

'Where should it go?'

'Front and centre. Where we'll see it every time we look

at the tree.' Lucy watched him hang it carefully. 'There. Perfect.'

They decorated slowly, talking about nothing and everything. James kept asking questions about ornaments, about traditions, about Christmas in 2025. Lucy explained whilst hanging lights and arranging baubles.

'Why are the lights shaped like icicles?' James asked, holding up a string of LED lights that dripped downward.

'Because someone decided droopy lights looked festive. Don't overthink it.'

'I'm being observant. There's a difference.'

'There really isn't.' She handed him more baubles. 'Here, make yourself useful. Hang these evenly around the tree. Not all clustered on one side like you're doing.'

'I'm creating visual balance.'

'You're creating a lopsided mess. Spread them out properly.'

James redistributed baubles whilst Lucy strung more lights. The tree slowly transformed from a bare pine to a festive centrepiece. Each addition brought more colour, more light, more warmth.

'What's this?' He held up a felt reindeer with a red nose and an expression of deep confusion.

'Rudolph the famous reindeer who guides Santa's sleigh through fog with his glowing nose. He came from a children's story in 1939.'

'We don't have famous reindeer with medical anomalies leading flying sleighs. We have Father Christmas coming down chimneys with a sack.'

'Wait until you hear about elves running a toy workshop at the North Pole.' Lucy grinned at his expression. 'One of the perks of time travel. You get to experience cultural developments all at once.'

'What a magnificent future I've chosen.'

'It is magnificent so embrace the absurdity.' She stood back to assess their work. 'There, now that looks properly Christmassy.'

The tree did look good. Lights twinkled cheerfully. Baubles caught and reflected the electric glow. The Victorian ornament hung front and centre, a bridge between two times and two lives.

'It's beautiful,' James said quietly.

Lucy found holly in the garden, and they hung it over doorways. She lit candles and placed them on mantels. Made the house warm and bright and unmistakably Christmas.

Evening fell. Through the window, Otley glowed with lights. Electric lights in every house, street lamps illuminating the roads, car headlights moving in steady streams. Modern Christmas, bright and electric and nothing like the Victorian version.

James stood at the window, looking out. 'Tomorrow is Christmas Day. The day I was supposed to die well, the day history says I died.'

'History can be wrong.' Lucy came to stand beside him. 'Are you afraid?'

'Terrified,' James admitted. 'I'm either still going to die tomorrow or I'm about to become a man with no past, no credentials, no identity. I'll have to start my entire life over.'

'We'll figure it out.'

'And what if it doesn't work? What if I can't adapt? What if I'm too old, too Victorian, too stuck in outdated practices? What if I stay here and end up useless?'

'Then you'll be a useless but hopefully alive Victorian in 2025 instead of a dead Victorian in 1885. Still an improvement.' Lucy took his hand. 'James, you're not going to fail. You're brilliant, you learned modern technology in days and adapted to the hospital like you'd been there for years. You'll figure out modern medicine because you're a doctor. It's who you are, regardless of the century, but it's not too late to change your mind.'

James looked at the passage. The darkness stretched away toward his Victorian life. His patients, his practice, his familiar world. Everything he'd known for thirty-five years.

Then he looked at Lucy, the electric lights behind her and the future, bright and impossible yet terrifying and wonderful.

'I'm not changing my mind.' His voice was steady, sure. He reached past her and pushed the bookcase closed firmly. The mechanism clicked, and the passage disappeared.

'There,' James said. 'Done. I'm staying.'

They stood in the library, electric light overhead, a decorated tree visible through the doorway. Just two people, together at last.

'What do we do now?' James asked.

'Now we eat something ridiculously Christmassy. Probably argue about Victorian decorating traditions versus modern ones. Stay up too late talking about the future.' Lucy smiled. 'Normal Christmas Eve things. Except with time travel and how to undertake identity fraud.'

'Sounds perfect.' James pulled her close. 'Thank you for believing in me.'

'Thank you for choosing to stay. Come on, I have mince pies.'

In the kitchen, Lucy heated mince pies in the microwave whilst James watched, still fascinated by the appliance that heated food with invisible radiation.

'These are quite good,' he said after his first bite. 'Not as good as Mrs Barker's, but acceptable.'

'Shop-bought versus homemade. We're doing well for last-minute Christmas preparations.' Lucy poured tea into mismatched mugs. 'To be fair, I had no plans for Christmas this year. You're a considerable improvement on sitting alone feeling sorry for myself.'

'Likewise. My Christmas plan was dying, which is admittedly quite low on the festivity scale.'

'Definitely low. We've significantly upgraded both our situations I hope.'

They sat at the kitchen table, eating mince pies and drinking tea whilst snow fell outside. Ordinary and extraordinary all at once.

'Tell me something about your future,' James said. 'Our future. What happens after Christmas Day?'

'Practically?'

'No, personally? What happens to us?'

'We figure it out as we go. You hopefully do not die and live here whilst you're studying and we see if this, us, is real or just the adrenaline of an impossible situation.' She met his eyes. 'I'm not naive enough to think falling in love in a week means we'll work forever. But I'm hopeful enough to want to try.'

'I want to try too. Very much.' James reached across the table to take her hand. 'Fair warning, I'm probably going to be difficult. Stubborn about learning new things. Frustrated when I don't understand modern concepts immediately. Possibly insufferable about historical accuracy in markets.'

'I'm counting on it. It keeps life interesting.'

'You're my reason to keep going.'

In 1885, in James's house, the gaslight would burn through the night. Mrs Barker would discover his letter on Christmas morning, Dr Fletcher would be contacted, and life would continue.

In 2025, in Lucy's inherited house, two people who shouldn't exist together made tea and ate mince pies and talked until dawn about medicine and plans and the logistics of creating a life from nothing.

Outside, snow began to fall. Soft flakes drifting down, covering 2025 Otley in white, and James and Lucy sat by the Christmas tree, watching lights twinkle on the Victorian bauble. Tomorrow would bring challenges, complications, difficulties neither of them could fully imagine.

But tonight was simple. Two people, one choice, infinite possibilities.

'To tomorrow,' Lucy said, raising her mug of tea.

'To tomorrow,' James echoed, clinking his mug against hers. 'To life.'

They drank to the future whilst snow fell outside, covering the past.

And somewhere in the house, if you listened very carefully, you might hear the faintest echo of magic. Feel a sense of time folding and unfolding. Or, a reminder that some things are meant to be, regardless of when they happen.

James Ashworth chose life on Christmas Eve 2025. And life, grateful and generous, chose him back.

EPILOGUE

Seven years later, Dr James Ashworth stood in the emergency department of Leeds General Infirmary, his stethoscope around his neck, his white coat crisp and professional. A qualified doctor once again. Forty-two years old, the oldest person in his graduating class, but he'd done it.

'Dr Ashworth?' A nurse appeared at his elbow. 'We've got a child in Bay Three. Suspected croup. Parents are terrified.'

'I'll go now.' James headed toward the bay, his training clicking into place automatically. Ancient skills from 1885 combined with modern knowledge from the 21st century. The best of both worlds.

The child was small, struggling to breathe, his parents hovering anxiously. James examined him carefully, noting the symptoms, assessing severity. In 1885, this child might have died. In 2025, it was treatable.

'He's going to be fine,' James told the parents. 'We'll give him medication to reduce the inflammation, monitor him overnight. But he'll recover fully.'

Relief flooded their faces. 'Thank you, doctor. Thank you so much.'

After his shift, James drove home to Otley. To the Victorian house that Lucy still owned and to the woman who'd saved his life and taught him to live.

Lucy was in the kitchen cooking dinner. Still not particularly skilled, but competent enough. She looked up when he entered, smiling.

'How was your day?'

'Terrifying but wonderful. I saved three lives before lunch. Saved them, with tools that work and knowledge that makes sense.' He kissed her hello.

'I'm proud of and I love you.'

'I love you too. Always will.'

They ate dinner together, talking about their days. Ordinary conversation in an ordinary kitchen. Two people who'd crossed time to find each other, now living an ordinary life filled with extraordinary love.

In the library, the bookcase stood unchanged. The passage had never reopened. Perhaps it never would.

But sometimes, late at night, if you stood very still, you might feel something. A shimmer. A whisper. A reminder that magic existed. That time could fold. That love was stronger than history.

James Ashworth vanished without a trace on Christmas Day 1885, according to the history books. Otley's unsolved mystery.

But James Ashworth lived. He thrived, loved and saved countless lives with modern medicine in modern times. He built an impossible life with an impossible woman who'd believed in him when he'd stopped believing in himself.

History was wrong. Love was right.

And that made all the difference.

… THE END

www.ingramcontent.com/pod-product-compliance
Lightning Source LLC
LaVergne TN
LVHW040152080526
838202LV00042B/3134